The Banker and The Dragon

Martin Lundqvist

Published by Martin Lundqvist, 2020.

THE BANKER AND THE DRAGON

First edition. May 10, 2020.

Written by Martin Lundqvist.

Chapter 1: The Honey Dragon, 2nd March 2021.

'Turkish Elvish Honey'

Chairman Jing Xi of the Columnist Party of China, CPOC, studied the jar in anticipation. He was a man of extravagant taste, and it didn't get fancier than this, buying honey that was worth its weight in gold. Jing smelled the honey, and the sensation took him a bit closer to heaven. He closed his eyes and Jing pictured himself on the top of the world, listening to serene music in a Tibetan temple on the top of a mountain.

The association with Tibet surprised Jing. He didn't care for the monks and their music. Furthermore, the party that he oversaw, had brutally subjugated the Tibetan people some decades earlier. 'Am I getting soft as my age advances?' Jing thought for a moment.

Jing brushed off the notion. He was approaching 67 years of age, but he was still a man of power, and in many ways in the prime of his life. The longest living emperor, the Qianlong emperor who had lived in the 18th century had lived until the age of 87. Jing, who had expertise in both Chinese medicine and modern medicine, strived to outlive that legendary emperor.

Jing grabbed a spoon and ingested a spoonful of the exquisite honey. It tasted as amazing as it smelled, but as the taste faded in his mouth, Jing felt dissatisfied and restless. Eating honey that cost more than the average annual salary in China hadn't resolved the issue that kept frustrating Jing and filled him with anger.

Jing felt that the people should worship him like they had worshipped the ancient emperors. Instead, his subjects were busy slandering him behind his back. How did the ungrateful masses dare to treat him like this? They should deify him for his leadership. During Jing's reign as the Chairman of the Columnist Party, China had risen to its rightful place as the centre of the world. Yet the topic of this month's column was an insult to his person. The WeChat voters had decided that this month's topic should be: 'How I intend to improve my character during the year of the Ox.'

This topic was nothing but dissent towards his leadership, and it was a dangerous column to write. He couldn't admit having character flaws, as he represented the state, and the state was faultless. But he couldn't be too arrogant either as that would contravene his promise to the people. Jing had promised the Chinese public a change when he reformed the Chinese Communist Party, CCP, into the Columnist Party of China, CPOC.

The name change of the party was Jing playing lip service to the Western world. This was to secure international trade that was crucial for his ambitions. Nothing had changed under his leadership, but at least he had given the people the chance to vote. Although Jing had restricted the popular vote to entail the topic of his monthly column in China Daily. This cosmetic change hadn't caused him any grief until this month.

Jing closed his laptop. He wouldn't write that article; the topic was beneath him. Instead, he would have sex to release his frustration. Jing's latest concubine, the 23-year-old winner of the National Chinese pageant, the stunning Min Li, had improved Jing's life in that aspect.

Jing summoned Min Li, and she told him that she would arrive in 30 minutes. Having summoned Min Li, Jing experienced restlessness and anticipation. He was 67 years old, and he was under a lot of stress. He needed to get a proper release, and he didn't want any violent mishaps. Covering up his violence towards previous concubines had stolen a lot of energy.

Jing took out a Ziplock bag that contained a powder. The powder was a mixture of Viagra and ground rhino horn, and it always worked on him. Jing believed in mixing the best of Chinese and western medicine, and he followed this thesis in many aspects of his life.

30 minutes later, Min Li entered Jing's residence, and she kneeled at his feet.

Min Li:

- You summoned me, Heavenly Master. How can I serve you?

Jing:

> - I didn't hire you for your intellect. So, shut up and use your mouth
> for something useful.

Min Li hesitated. She hated the way that Jing treated her, but she didn't dare to argue with the supreme leader. Reluctantly, she kneeled next to the Jing and unbuttoned his exquisite silk pants.

Jing:

> - Good dog. Obey your master.

Having said this, Jing sighed as his young mistress gave him fellatio. If it could only release his anger, but it was in vain. Jing wanted to punch the bitch for doing it wrong, but he controlled himself. Instead, he took her from behind and he felt relieved when he came. Now, he could send her away while keeping his self-respect.

As he had finished, Jing threw Min's clothes to her and spoke:

> - Wash up and make sure to look good for tomorrow's photoshoot. I
> don't want any more stuff-ups!

> - Dismissed.

Min Li, who struggled to contain her tears, got dressed and rushed to leave Jing's residence.

Jing got seated by his computer. He checked if the advanced AI that supervised the Chinese population had found any new enemies. It had. Jing cursed at himself. Of course, there would be dissenters in a country with 1.4 billion inhabitants. The ancient emperors were wise, secluding themselves in their forbidden cities. That way, they had never faced the opinions of regular citizens. Jing knew that he shouldn't look, but he couldn't help himself. Knowing which enemies, the AI had identified, was his drug, and he could not break the vicious addiction.

Jing's eyes got fixated on the file of Eileen Lu. Her file said that she was a 28-year-old lawyer and civil rights activist. Eileen had recently got one of his enemies, Ming Shebao, acquitted in the people's court of Xuwan. It was unbelievable that the courts in HIS country had acquitted one of his enemies, but it was an issue that he needed to deal with. Jing stared at Eileen's photo for a long time.

Eileen's beauty captivated Jing, and he knew that he needed to own her. Yet, Jing's power wasn't absolute. While he could eliminate the enemies of the republic, he couldn't kidnap and rape people on his whim. The rest of his party would never allow it. But he would own Eileen one way or the other, and she would regret defying him. Filled with rage, Jing picked up his expensive jar of honey and threw it against the wall, splashing honey across the room.

Chapter 2: Another Win for Freedom, 5th of March 2021.

"...**A**nd because of the disclaimer regarding fictional content, Mary Sheng didn't break any laws when she drew a sad bear looking at an empty honey jar."

Eileen Lu finished her statement and she corrected her glasses. She wore the glasses as a fashion statement, and because she knew that the judge on the case, Feng Woo, liked goofy women. Eileen looked at Feng and gave him a pretence innocent-look, knowing that she had him in her back pocket.

Feng Woo cleared his throat and spoke.

- You raise some valid points, Miss Lu. I am willing to drop this case if Miss Sheng, apologises to Chairman Xi about the resemblance between the sad bear and our Supreme Leader.

"Please don't make a scene!" Eileen thought as she leaned over to her client and whispered in Mary Sheng's ear.

- Please take the plea bargain. I have done everything I can to save you.

Feng Woo:

- Don't whisper to your client. Everyone deserves to hear the advice that you are giving your client.

Eileen:

- I am sorry for my insolence, Magistrate Woo. I merely recommended my client to accept your gracious offer.

Feng Woo:

- But, if that is the case, how can we be sure that the client shows remorse for her thoughtlessness?

Mary Sheng interjected:

- Please, Magistrate Woo. I want nothing more than letting the Chinese people know how sorry I am.

Feng smirked at Mary and replied:

- Good. How lucky that we have a camera crew filming the proceedings

- Read these lines. We will record until you get it right. I want to see heartfelt remorse on the video. I don't want to see a woman who is lying to save her life. Can you do that?

Mary nodded, and one of Feng's aides handed Mary a note. Mary read the note a few times, and she started crying. Mary:

- I am ready to film.

clap clap
Feng clapped his hands and he taunted:

- Excellent. Get ready, team. Let's produce a new masterpiece.

An AV-crew entered the room and they rigged a video shoot. A few minutes later, Mary was ready to confess. Mary looked into the camera with her teary eyes and spoke:

- I want to say sorry to all the people of China who I offended with my talentless drawing. Being a true patriot, I cannot stop thinking about Chairman Xi and it influenced my drawing. The empty jar symbolises how poor China was, before our saviour lifted our people out of poverty. I am truly grateful for how merciful the court has been towards an old woman like I.

Feng:

- Cut!

- Such terrible acting. But I cannot back down on my word. Get out of here you wretched cow! Dismissed!

Eileen acted decisively and pulled Mary out of the room to avoid a confrontation. When they were outside of the courthouse Mary shouted at Eileen.

- You destroyed my legacy, Eileen. I should have stood strong and taken my unjust punishment. Instead, I looked like a snivelling coward, praising Jing Xi and this travesty of a court.

- I'd rather spend some time in prison, but you stopped me. Why?

Eileen:

- I saved your life. While the court sentence wouldn't have killed you, you would have had an accident within the next year. As is customary for people that anger Jing Xi.

- Faking an apology was the only way to save you.

Mary Sheng calmed down and she covered her face with her hands. After a while she spoke:

- You're right, Eileen. Thank you for saving my life.

Eileen smiled and replied:

- That's my job. As your lawyer, I am here for you.

Mary:

- You were the only one. Of the millions that saw and liked my drawing on WeChat, you were the only one who protected me when things got tough.

Eileen:

- That is, unfortunately, human nature and the reason that Chairman Xi can continue his tyranny.

- What are your plans now?

Mary:

- I'll go home to Xuwan. I'll delete my online presence and spend my last year's nursing my grandchildren.

Eileen:

- Best of luck to you. I'll come to visit you, Xuwan is beautiful in spring.

Mary:

- Don't worry about this old hag!

- Focus on yourself, Eileen. Find a rich handsome man, and raise a happy family.

Eileen didn't reply and Mary entered a cab that took her to the train station. Eileen went home and she poured herself some herbal tea. She felt empty. While she had won in the sense that she had saved her client, she had destroyed Mary's sense of pride and bowed to the tyrant Jing Xi. Most of all she felt shame. Like everyone else, she loathed and feared the dictator. Yet, she did nothing and she instructed her clients to bow to the tyranny. Eileen wished that her time for bravery would come, but for now, she could only focus on her life and finding that prince charming!

Chapter 3: Royal Casino. 7th March 2021.

Jared Pond was pulling his hand through his long blonde hair while sipping his Espresso Martini. Jared's expensive brand name tuxedo was getting tight and he knew that he needed to go back to Australia for training and detox soon. It didn't cut it, to be an agent for the Royal Australian Kangaroo Intelligence (RAKI) while being unfit.

The lack of fitness came with the territory. Jared's greatest strengths lay in his sharp observation ability, and poker skills. His assignment here at Royal Casino in Monaco combined those strengths. While the poker playing was a way to pass the time, Jared also had a mission in Monaco. He needed to investigate if the leader of the Global Health Association (GHA), Theodore Ahmadi, took bribes from the Chinese government.

Jared got distracted from the poker when his latest fling, the Italian femme fatale Celeste Florentino tapped him on his back.

- Hi Jared, how nice to see you again. Are you winning at the tables today?

Jared:

- I think I just did.

Jared turned towards the others, gathered his chips, and spoke:

- Well played, gentlemen. I need to focus on the lady now.

Jared got up and smiled at Celeste:

- Would you like some Dom Perignon to celebrate the occasion?

Celeste smiled seductively at Jared and replied:

- Of course, there is not a better way to get a woman excited for the evening.

'I wish there was,' Jared thought to himself, but instead he replied:

- Come with me, Celeste.

Having said this, Jared put his hand on Celeste's back and he walked her to the bar. "Keep the change!" Jared said as he paid for the exquisite champagne with a 500-euro gambling marker.
Celeste:

- That's a very generous tip, Jared.

Jared:

- I can't bring money to the grave, and in my line of work, one never knows when the grave is due.

Celeste:

- What exactly do you do for work, Jared?

Jared:

- Shh, we are too early in our connection to ruin the mystique.

Hearing this, Celeste grabbed one of the strawberries that came with the champagne, and bit it seductively.

- I agree. You know how to behave yourself, Mr Pond.

Jared reflected over why Celeste addressed him by his last name, but he soon found a more pressing matter. His target, Theodore Ahmadi, entered the casino, and he got seated by a table occupied by a Chinese businessman.

Jared had seen the same procedure take place several times in the last week. Every day, Theodore got seated at a table and won a large sum from a Chinese man, who subsequently left the casino. Since it had happened five days in a row, it was not a coincidence.

Jared decided to observe the transaction while sitting at the same table, he handed Celeste his room key and spoke.

- I got to work, honey. Meet me at my room, 407, in one hour. Keep the champagne cool and everything else hot.

Celeste:

- You can't treat me like that. I am not a prostitute!

Jared pretended to drop 1000 euros in chips and he replied:

- Oh, how clumsy of me. I just dropped a thousand Euros. They are yours if you pick them up.

Jared looked at Celeste in disappointment as she got down on the floor and picked up the chips. She had failed both his tests, and he realised that she wasn't the one for him. On the bright side, her body was luscious and she would keep him busy tonight. This wouldn't have happened if she had splashed the champagne in his face and taken off.

Jared walked over to Theodore's table where the Ethiopian had won 50,000 euros from the anonymous Chinese businessman who was getting ready to leave.

Jared approached Theodore and spoke:

- Do you mind if I join you?

Theodore:

- I was about to leave.

Jared:

- Don't be like that. You just arrived and luck is favouring you tonight.

While saying this, Jared glanced at the Chinese man who was rushing to get away from the table.

Theodore seemed hesitant, but at last, he decided to stay:

- Very well, Mr?

Jared:

- Pond. Jared Pond.

Theodore:

- Ahmadi, Theodore Ahmadi.
- I will play you, Mr Pond.

Jared:

- May the best man win.

Jared and Theodore played for a while until Jared started missing Celeste's warm body and decided to lure his Ethiopian adversary into a trap.

Theodore flustered when he realised that he had lost 100,000 Euros.

Theodore:

- Fuck. Well played Mr Pond. I shouldn't have overextended my luck!

Jared smirked at Theodore and replied:

- I am sure that money will drop down from the sky for you again. If not, you still have the 200,000 that you won from the other Chinese gentlemen. I bid thee farewell.

Jared got up, collected his chips, and bowed theatrically as he walked towards the cashier to deposit his winnings. After that, he walked up to room 407, for a steamy night with Celeste. She had failed his tests so far, and she was unlikely to win his heart. But with a body like hers, she had won his body for the night!

Chapter 4: Pierre Beaumont is Planning his Ascension. 10th March 2021.

The World Bank deputy director, Pierre Beaumont, was enjoying a sumptuous dinner at the 'Le Comer Paradise' restaurant in Hague. World Economic Forum was coming up in a few days, and Pierre had an urgent matter on hand. The world had cooled down, as the sun had entered a Global Solar Minimum which had lowered the average temperature by 0.2 degrees.

This caused Pierre a headache as he had planned to become the CEO of the World Bank through his active stance against climate change. This issue would become less important if the global temperatures were falling. However, Pierre had a solution to his predicament. Pierre had convinced that fool, Martin Orchard, to murder Pierre's rival at the World Bank, Chakri Apinya. Pierre planned to blame the murder on the Buddhist leader Arhat Somchai. Because the world needed distractions so no-one asked about global warming!

Pierre stroke his balding head, and he studied CIA Agent James Winter who approached him. James was tall and muscular, with a perfect set of light brown hair and lively eyes. Compared to Pierre he looked like a Greek god. Pierre brushed off his complex, Pierre was wealthy and he had unmatched intellect. Particularly since the incident in Nepal, the previous year.

In Nepal, Pierre, James and a group of travellers had lost their way during a blizzard and found an ancient alien temple. In the temple, they had found alien technology that elevated their intellects and gave them impressive abilities. The monocle that Pierre often wore, contained this alien technology.

James got seated and Pierre whispered.

- We should not both wear the monocle at the same time. It looks too conspicuous.

James shrugged his shoulders and replied:

- Who cares? People are too busy staring at their phones, following the vain celebrity culture, to notice.

Pierre felt irritated by James' reply, but he didn't say anything. He considered taking off his monocle but he decided against it. Pierre was the vice director of the World Bank, soon to be director, and he couldn't give in to a lowly CIA agent. Pierre changed the topic.

- Our subsidiary, Xeng Fao Technologies, won the tender to maintain the new 'Eternal Safeguard" AI in China.

James:

- Perfect. Jing Xi is obsessed with using that AI to control his population. If we control China's AI, we control the World.

Pierre:

- Exactly. We need a new crisis, by the way.

James:

- What's wrong with Climate Change?

Pierre:

- The sun has entered a Grand Solar Minimum, and Earth is getting colder.

James:

- That won't last forever. I am sure it will get hotter at some point.

Pierre:

- I'd rather not wait for that to happen.

James:

- So, what do you suggest? That we start another war in the Middle East?

Pierre:

- Wars are a risky business. I don't want to destroy the world that I seek to dominate.

- Regardless, the World Bank cannot win a regular war. Our best hope is economic warfare.

James:

- How do you intend to conduct economic warfare?

Pierre:

- I am not sure, yet. But opportunities will arise, as they always do, when I am looking for them.

A waiter attended the table, and James ordered a Budweiser with his thick American accent. When the waiter had left, James turned towards Pierre and spoke:

- So, Pierre. Tell me about your plan for disposing of Chakri Apinya?

Pierre smiled. He didn't expect that he would need the assistance of the CIA on this matter, but It was always good to have a backup plan. For the next 20 minutes, Pierre hinted James about his plan, without revealing the exact details. While the CIA was a useful ally, Pierre wasn't foolish enough to trust them!

Chapter 5: The discovery of the Hei Bai Virus, 27th March 2021.

Chairman Jing Xi, was finishing his monthly column for the China Daily. He emailed the document to the editor, and he slammed his computer against the floor in frustration. He had hated writing the column about how he intended to improve his character traits in 2021 but it was part of the societal contract. One of his obligations as the chairman of the Columnist Party of China was to write an article that the people requested, once a month. Jing's promise for self-improvement was to stop importing expensive honey and instead ensure that China produced the best honey in the world.

To produce the best honey in the world, Jing had travelled to Elephant Hill in the Guilin region of China. The caves, vegetation, and climate of this location should create the perfect blend of honey. Jing closed his eyes and he envisioned how this perfect blend would taste.

Jing's secretary, Biyu Sang, interrupted him in his thoughts.

- Chairman Xi. Theodore Ahmadi from the Global Health Association will meet with you shortly.

Jing:

- Why is that dog coming? Why didn't you cancel the meeting?

Biyu:

- I couldn't cancel it as you told me about your Guilin trip yesterday, and Theodore was already on his way to China.

Jing:

- Very well. I forgive your incompetence. But keep making mistakes
and it will cost you dearly.

Biyu:

- Thank you for having mercy on this dumb and useless woman. You
are the most gracious leader that China has ever seen.

Biyu bowed, turned around and quickly left Jing's office. 'Pathetic woman.
She fucked up, I forgave her, and yet she cried.' Jing thought.

Jing leaned back in his massage chair and he turned on some meditative
music. Jing recalled that he was meant to discuss China's aid in alleviating an
Ebola outbreak in central Africa. But this was of no concern to Jing, so instead,
Theodore would have to accompany him during his pursuit to find for the perfect honey making location. The only way to make his lapdog obey him, was to
treat him as such. Jing leaned back into his chair and fell asleep.

BIYU SANG

- Chairman Xi, Theodore Ahmadi has arrived.

Jing opened his eyes, Biyu was standing on the other side of the desk. She
looked tense, as if she was anticipating that Jing would attack her. This didn't
come to pass, Jing had experienced great dreams, envisioning a honey degusta-
tion while his concubine Min Li was massaging him. He couldn't be angry after
such a pleasant dream. Jing Xi spoke

- Very well, let him in.

Theodore entered the room, and Jing struggled to hide his contempt for
the scruffy African man, whom he would have to interact with for the next few
hours. Jing had preferred to appoint a Chinese citizen to be the GHA direc-

tor, but an African would have more credibility among Jing's western enemies. Theodore spoke:

- Greetings Chairman Xi. Can I expect China's help to resolve the Ebola epidemic in Central Africa?

Jing:

- Is this a real epidemic or are you merely trying to extort more money?

Theodore:

- It is a real epidemic. I wouldn't bother you otherwise. You have been very generous to me and my country.

Jing:

- Very well. I want you to get down on the floor, begging me for the money.

Theodore:

- I cannot do that. I am the leader of an important global organisation. We are equals.

Hearing Theodore's objections, Jing lost his temper. He picked up a vase and he threw it at the floor next to Theodore. As the vase shattered, Jing roared:

- You are nothing but my dog. I put you where you are and I can put you somewhere else. No-one will ever know what happened to you!

- Now kneel and beg for my forgiveness.

Being a pathetic and corrupt lapdog, Theodore got down to the ground, kissed Jing's shoes and pleaded:

- Please forgive me, Heavenly Master Xi. Please have mercy on the poor souls in Central Africa who cannot develop enough, to deal with their local diseases.

Jing spat next Theodore and replied:

- Get up, you dog. You have swayed my heart. Speak to my ministers and the Chinese Empire will save your sorry continent, for now.

Theodore:

- Thank you, Master Xi. God bless your kindness and grace.

Jing:

- I care little for deities and other superstitions.

- But since you are here, you'll follow me on an important mission today.

Theodore:

- What do you need me to do, Chairman Xi?

Jing:

- You're coming with me to the caves near Elephant Hill. You can fill me in on your Ebola epidemic while we are in the car.

Jing picked up his phone, organised his car, and left his office, with Theodore as his obedient dog in tow.

JING WAS ENJOYING THE view from the Elephant Hill lookout. He would make sure to get photos of him and Theodore, that could accompany the official narrative. Jing cringed as the burst of photo flashes struck his face, and he had to pretend to smile and treat Theodore as his equal. In the past, the emperor of China had been revered like a god, yet Jing had to pretend to be equal to his African henchman.

"Don't get any ideas!" Jing whispered to Theodore, who looked away. After finishing the press conference, Jing and his entourage started walking to a nearby cave. The cave was perfect. Jing had never been to the cave where the Turkish Elvish Honey was made, but his intuition told him that this place would do the job. As Jing and Theodore traversed deeper into the cave, Jing heard a cough echoing. This was followed by a male voice wheezing "Help me."

One of Jing's bodyguards, Chao Li, approached him and whispered into his ear:

- Chairman Xi. We found a very ill man. This place is not safe. We better get you back to safety.

Jing gave Chao a stern look and replied.

- I am the master of this country. The truth cannot be concealed from me. I want to see the man who is wheezing.

Chao:

- Understood. Put on this facemask and follow me.

Jing put on his facemask, turned towards Theodore and spoke:

- Come with me. As the leader for the Global Health Association, you can help with the diagnosis.

Theodore:

- But I don't have a facemask.

Jing:

- Well, that's a shame. Shouldn't the leader for the GHA always have one in his pocket? Pray to your gods that the disease is not infectious.

Jing didn't wait for Theodore's response. Instead, he ventured forth until he reached the source of the wheezing.

Jing stared in shock and awe at the sick man. The man had a layer of fungus that covered his body and gave off the impression that he was covered in bark. The man's eyes were blood sprained and he smelled of faeces.

The diseased man got up on his feet and tried to approach Jing:

- Chairman Xi. You must help me. The pain is unbearable.

Jing didn't have the time to respond as a multitude of bullets ended the disease-stricken man's life. Jing turned around and gave Chao a disapproving look:

- Why did you shoot that man, Chao?

Chao:

- He was posing a threat to you, Heavenly Master.

Jing:

- Bloody fool. You could have knocked him out. We lost an excellent opportunity to examine this man for our biological weapons program.

- Anyways. Let's get out of here. Get our scientists to come here and examine the man and the cave. Leave no stone unturned.

Having said this, Jing left the cave. As his car drove him and Theodore back to the banquet hall, for a state dinner, Jing spoke:

- I hope that you realise that nothing of this happened?

Theodore:

- As far as I am concerned, you took me to a beautiful lookout and then you shared your passion for honey-making with me. Nothing else happened.

Jing:

- We are on the same page. Keep being on the same page, so I don't have to close your book.

Having said this, Jing plugged in headphones to listen to meditative music and ignored Theodore for the rest of the drive.

Chapter 6: Jing finds out about his Hei Bai virus infection, 4th April 2021.

- I have some bad news and some good news.

Jing's personal doctor, The Chinese Minster for Health, Dr Song Bao, revealed.

Jing studied his doctor. As if it wasn't bad enough to be back in the polluted shithole Beijing, he now also had to face some bad news? Jing spoke:

- Tell me the good news first. Anything to lighten up my life in this dreary city!

Song:

- We found the cause of death for the man who died in the cave near Elephant Hill. We have isolated a sample of the virus. We have never seen anything like it!

Jing:

- Excellent. This will be invaluable to our future bioweapon research!
- What is the bad news?

Song:

- The blood samples that we took from you and your entourage, show that you are all infected.

Hearing this, Jing sunk in his seat and despair overwhelmed him. He had seen the agony of the dying man in the cave, and this was not the way that he wanted to go. But what if he was immune? Like the vast majority had been during the previous year's Coronavirus outbreak? Jing decided to hope for that outcome. If he was immune nothing would happen, and if he was infected, he would be gone. In that case, it didn't matter to him if he brought a lot of others with him to the afterlife.

Jing:

- Doctor Bao. Make sure to quarantine everyone that was in the Elephant Hill cave. Don't tell anyone else about this.

Song:

- Understood, Chairman Xi.

Jing:

- Has anyone gotten any symptoms from the virus yet?

Song:

- No, everyone is healthy so far.

Jing

- Good. Extract and prepare a large batch of the virus. We need to test it on our Uighur prisoners, to find out more about it.

- Dismissed, Doctor Bao.

As Song Bao left the room, Jing experienced mixed feelings of anticipation and worry. He worried that he would succumb to the terrible fate that befell the man in the cave. But at the same time, he felt excitement. With a bit of luck, he could weaponise this new virus and use it to destroy the Western economies once and for all.

Chapter 7: Jared Pond receives a new mission, 10th April 2021.

Jared Pond was finishing another gruelling fitness session at the HMAS Kuttabul navy base in Sydney. Since his return to Australia, a few weeks earlier, he had pushed himself to the limit every day. The results were starting to show. Yet again, Jared looked like an agent from the movies, rather than an alcoholic with a gambling addiction. Speaking of gambling, the commander of the base had forbidden Jared from playing poker, as his many wins caused a lot of tension among the men.

Jared felt surprised when his commander at RAKI, Greg Steel, approached him at the gym.

Greg:

- Hi Jared. I got a new mission for you.

Jared:

- Why are you telling me like this? Wouldn't a meeting at your office be more appropriate?

Greg:

- I am going to New York tomorrow morning, and you're coming with me.

Jared:

- What is this about?

Greg:

- There are rumours about the Chinese dictatorship conducting medical tests on their Uighur prisoners.

Jared:

- I am sorry, but I wouldn't be suitable for a mission in China. I am not Chinese, and I don't speak the language.

Greg:

- I know. That's why you are coming with me to New York. We tracked the person who posted the accusations against the Chinese government.

Jared:

- Was the source believable or was it another tin foil conspiracist?

Greg:

- That is your mission to find out. The woman who posted the article was Eileen Lu. She is a Chinese civil rights lawyer who is currently attending a UN civil rights conference in New York city.

Jared:

- I see. And what would my mission entail?

Greg:

- You do what you do best. Seduce her and get her to share her secrets with you. Only then can we know whether she is trustworthy or not.

Jared sighed:

- Hey Greg. Stop treating me like a man-whore, please.

Greg smirked:

- Isn't that the way you have treated yourself for the last decade?

Jared:

- Fair call. At least tell me if she is a good sort.

Greg:

- I leave that for you to decide.

Having said this, Greg handed Jared a photo of Eileen. Jared studied the photo for a while. Eileen looked cute and quirky, but would she be the kind of woman that would fall for his charms? Jared pushed the thought aside. He had an obligation to use his talents to serve his country and save his fellow citizens. Whatever the Chinese dictatorship was planning, the world needed to know and prepare for the worst.
Jared:

- Very well, I'll come with you to New York. Hopefully, I can work
  my magic on this Eileen woman.

Greg:

- Excellent. See you tomorrow for the 9 AM flight to New York.

After saying this, Greg left the building and Jared prepared himself mentally for the upcoming mission. He stared at Eileen's picture even though he knew that he shouldn't. He needed to stay calm and collected for the mission ahead of him, otherwise, things could end badly. Jared went home, showered, packed his bag, and went to sleep early to be ready for the next mission.

Chapter 8: Pond, Jared Pond. 12th April 2021.

Eileen Lu stared at her computer screen. There were no new emails, which was a relief. A lot of emails would be an indication that she had been exposed. It would be dangerous if people on the Internet, as well as the CPOC, knew that she had spread leaked videos from the Uighur concentration camps. The world needed to know what was going on, but Eileen loved living too much for the Columnist Party of China to know that she had exposed them. All governments hated when people exposed their crimes, but the CPOC hated it more than most governments.

Eileen looked at the asylum request that she had written to the American government. She was certain that they would grant her request because of her relative fame as a human rights advocate. But if she sought asylum in the USA, she would abandon her people and become a mouthpiece for American propaganda. Eileen didn't want to help the USA against her mother nation, she wanted to liberate the Chinese people from Jing's tyranny.

Eileen made up her mind. She threw her asylum application in the bin, and she prepared herself for today's seminary. Open dialogue and genuine discussion were the only ways to progress humankind and Eileen wanted to play her role. Eileen closed her laptop, put it in her bag and started walking towards the Downtown Conference Centre in New York.

As Eileen left her hotel, she noticed the man who observed her from across the road. He was athletic, had long blonde hair, and he looked like your run of the mill superhero from the movies. Eileen would have loved if he approached her in a cocktail bar, but having him stalk her at 8 AM was outright creepy. Had someone sent this man to hurt her? Eileen shook off the notion. The man didn't look like he a Columnist Party henchman, and besides, he stood out too much to be a suitable assassin.

Eileen stopped staring at the man, and she set out to walk her conference. She got to a pedestrian crossing, and the red light stressed her. Eileen was giving a presentation in the morning, and she would hate to be late. Worse yet, she couldn't shake off the feeling that people were following her.

Splash

Someone bumped Eileen from behind and splashed warm latte over her white blazer. 'Fucking hell, why today out of all days?' Eileen thought and turned around. What she saw petrified her. The blonde man, which she had noticed before, was the one who had bumped her.

Jared:

- I am so sorry, how clumsy of me!

Eileen shook her head and sneered at Jared:

- Clumsy? I saw that you were checking me out when I left the hotel. Is this how men try to connect with women in New York City?

Jared leaned in and whispered:

- I am sorry, Eileen. My name is Pond, Jared Pond, and I need to talk to you. It's important.

Eileen wouldn't have it and she replied:

- Okay, Mr Pond Jared Pond. I have to give an important presentation in one hour. And you ruined my blazer. Buzz off and book an appointment like everyone else.

The light turned green, Eileen slapped Jared, and she rushed to cross the street.

Eileen's rejection left Jared dumbfounded. Eileen's slap had stung but the rejection had stung more. Had he lost his touch with women after all these years, or was Eileen a special case? On the bright side, she had told him to book an appointment, so that was what he would do.

JARED POND WAS SIPPING an Espresso Martini in the upmarket cocktail bar, The Aviary NYC. His tailor-made tuxedo emphasized his great physique and sophisticated style.

"You cannot enter this establishment with those clothes. Please refer to our dress code, madam" Jared heard the doorman say this to some uncultured peasant. Jared looked in the direction of the entrance and he realised that the uncultured peasant was his appointment for the evening. Somehow, Eileen Lu thought that it was suitable to enter an upmarket venue dressed in jeans, sneakers and a T-shirt with a cartoon character.

Jared ran towards the entrance and intervened:

- It's okay, Michael. Eileen is with me. Please let her in.

Michael the Doorman:

- Sorry, Mr Pond. I need to uphold the dress code of this establishment.

Jared:

- But don't you have any suitable attire for the lady in the coatroom?

Michael nodded and ran off. A minute later he returned with an expensive ladies' fur coat.

Michael:

- Please wear this, Ms Eileen.

Eileen shook her head, but she agreed to put on the fur coat, which had been there since the winter months.

Jared:

- Can I get you a drink, Eileen? This place has a great selection of champagnes and cocktails.

Eileen:

- I would like a peppermint tea. I won't be staying, and I don't drink when I need to work the next day. Thanks for offering Mr Pond Jared Pond.

Jared:

- It's just Jared Pond.

Eileen:

- Why didn't you say it like that before then?

Jared:

- Never mind.

Jared walked up to the bar and he ordered two teapots with peppermint tea. He couldn't recall the last time that he drank tea, but he had to be flexible and drink what the situation required.

As the waiter arrived with the tea, Jared poured tea for himself and Eileen. As Eileen sipped the tea, she spoke:

- So, Mr Pond, who are you working for and what do you want?

Jared realised that he had lost his touch and he decided to give an honest reply:

- I am working for RAKI and I am investigating whether you are a credible source when it comes to the Uighur camps.

Eileen:

- Excuse me for not knowing every abbreviation in the spy community. RAKI?

Jared:

- Royal Australian Kangaroo Intelligence.

Eileen:

- For future reference, you should probably use the full name instead of the abbreviation.

Jared didn't comment on Eileen's statement. Although it was a bit hurtful that she didn't recognise the fame of his workplace, he had to focus on the mission.
Jared:

- So, the videos you uploaded. Who is the source and do you know what the Columnist Party injects prisoners with?

Eileen:

- I do trust the source but I won't reveal him to any spy. There is no reason for me to trust that the Australian government wouldn't sell him out to Jing Xi, as your spineless prime minister is licking Jing's boots. As for the injections I have no idea. But I doubt that it is for the benefit of the prisoners.

Jared reflected over Eileen's statement. That she didn't trust Australia's prime minister Scurry Morrissett, also known as Scummo, proved that she was of sound character and a sane mind.
Jared:

- Very well. I think this is all for today. Let's keep in touch. While I cannot speak for our prime minister, I am an advocate for protecting the Chinese people against Jing's tyranny.

Eileen shook her head:

- I rather not keep in touch. I don't want the Columnist Party to use my connections with an Australian spy to discredit me. Thank you for the tea, Mr Pond.

Pow

Jared was about to reply, when a punch knocked him off his chair.

Seeing the stars, Jared recognised his opponent, Marcel Blanco, a drug smuggler for the Colombian Juarez Cartel.

Marcel yelled at Jared:

- Puta de Madre. Why did you fuck my wife!

Jared reflected over Marcel's statement for a second. He didn't know who Marcel's wife was, but presumably, the act of copulation was to satisfy his own raging masculine needs.

Jared sprung to his feet and replied:

- I am sorry, but who is your wife?

Marcel screamed:

- You motherfucker! I'll kill you!

Having said this, Marcel swung a bottle after Jared.

Jared dodged the bottle, and then he kicked Marcel at the side of his knee. This dropped Marcel to a crouching position. Jared picked up a chair and swung it at the head of Marcel, knocking the Colombian unconscious.

Jared shouted at the unconscious Marcel:

- I still don't know who your wife is, Marcel!

After this, he corrected his bowtie and ran after Eileen. He caught up with her at the elevator.

Jared:

- Sorry about that. How are you spending the rest of your night?

Eileen:

- As far away from you as possible!

Jared:

- I just saved your life. That man attacked us.

Eileen:

- He attacked you. I had nothing to do with it. You are nothing but trouble. Goodnight, Mr Pond.

As Jared was driven to police custody, he reflected over Eileen's words. Was he the greatest agent that Australia had to offer, or was he a sex-addicted jerk that ended up in stupid fights? He couldn't come up with the answer to that philosophical question, but he did know one thing. He had a terrible headache.

Chapter 9: What an Embarrassment, Jared! 14th April 2021.

Jared Pond was sitting on a Qantas flight back to Australia. His mission had been a failure. He hadn't managed to seduce Eileen, and he had got himself arrested due to the altercation in the cocktail bar.

Jared's boss, Greg Steel, who sat next to him in the business class of the flight, decided to discuss the matter. Greg:

- What a debacle, Jared. All this because you couldn't keep your dick in your pants!

Jared:

- Stop moralising. You were the one who sent me to seduce Eileen in the first place.

Greg:

- That didn't work out, did it?

- Instead, you got into a bar fight because of your latest indiscretions with that Celeste Florentino woman.

Jared:

- You should be thankful that I wasn't seriously injured.

Greg:

- Well, then I wouldn't have to call Scurry Morrissette and plead him
to call Deidrick Dump to get you out of jail.

- We are a secret intelligence service. The secrecy part fails if I have
to get you out of jail because of your stupid private fights.

Jared:

- I apologise, Greg.

Greg:

- Too little and too late. We will have to reconsider your position
with RAKI.

Hearing this, came like a heavy burden on Jared's chest. Serving Australia
was all he knew, and he didn't know what he would do with himself if he lost
the job. He had no remaining family, he was unable to keep a long-term part-
ner, and he would get restless without the danger of his job.
Jared:

- Please give me another chance, Greg. I live for this job.

Greg:

- I will discuss your employment with Scurry when we return to Australia. For now, don't discuss this debacle with anyone.

Jared sighed and sat silent for a while. He closed his eyes, and he saw the
cute and quirky smile of Eileen Lu. He knew that she was genuine and telling
the truth and he couldn't get her out of his mind. Eileen's rejection of him was
a testament of her integrity, and Jared knew that he needed her.
Jared:

- Eileen is telling the truth. Jing Xi is up to some more villainy.

Greg shrugged his shoulders and replied:

- Oh really? What a shame that you stuffed up your mission so we won't get the chance to verify it.

- We have a sixteen-hour flight ahead of us. Please be quiet. I am intending to get some sleep.

Having said this, Greg put on a set of noise-cancelling earphones and a blindfold to ignore Jared.

Jared sighed. What a terrible mission. He was about to lose his job, and worse yet, he had become obsessed with a woman who rejected him. Following Greg's example, Jared put on his noise-cancelling earphones, started a playlist with jazz music, and closed his eyes.

Chapter 10: Jing has a realisation about the Hei Bai virus. 20th April 2021.

Jing Xi was experiencing mixed feelings. As it turned out, none of the 50,000 Uyghurs that his men had infected with the virus had developed any symptoms. On the bright side, this meant that his infection was unlikely to kill him.

Jing studied his latest blood test. The Hei Bai virus was still dormant in his body, but it seemed to not do anything to him. On the other hand, he hadn't developed antibodies to it either. What a bizarre virus.

Jing put his blood test aside, and he opened a bag of Brazil nuts. He hadn't eaten Brazil nuts for years, but it was good thing to have some variety in his diet. Jing picked up a handful of nuts and he started chewing on them, when his secretary, Biyu Sang, called him over the intercom.

- Chairman Xi. Vice-Chancellor Chi Wang requests that you come with him to the cabinet finance meeting.

Jing got irritated with Biyu. She needed to learn her place and not speak to him like that. Jing calmed down. He knew that Biyu was stuck between a rock and a hard place as she couldn't reject the Vice Chancellor's commands. Thus, it was Chi Wang that he needed to put into place! Jing put away the nuts and replied.

- Tell him that I am on my way.

Having said this, Jing picked up a flower vase and chucked it into the wall. On his way to the meeting, he spoke to Biyu:

- Biyu, you better clean up the vase that you made me break in my office. Don't anger me any more today!

JING LISTENED TO CHANCELLOR Chi Wang who described how the previous year's Coronavirus outbreak had benefitted the Chinese dictatorship. That crisis had been a stroke of genius. Shortly after the virus had struck China. Jing and his comrades had found out the truth, that the virus was extremely contagious but not very virulent. By concealing this fact, Jing and his politburo had declared that China had conquered the epidemic. They had quadrupled their wealth through trading on the international markets that had collapsed due to unfounded fears.

But the Coronavirus outbreak was over, and the world would be sceptical if a similar virus were to arise. Jing needed a new plan to enrichen himself and weaken his enemies.

Chi Wang:

- So, by selling our US treasury bonds on the 23rd of March 2020 and buying shares at the same time, we doubled our wealth.

Suddenly, Jing felt sick. Had anyone in the politburo poisoned him? He realised that he hadn't touched any of the food or beverage in the meeting room. Jing coughed violently and got up.

Chi Wang:

- Chairman Xi. Are you okay? Should I call our doctors?

Jing shook his head, and he exited the room. "I need to get to my office and contact Dr Song Bao," He thought. This was easier said than done. Jing was struggling to walk upright and the room became blurry. On top of that, his skin had a burning itch.

"Where is Biyu?" Jing thought, and he soon found his answer as he stumbled over Biyu in his office. Biyu stared at Jing in terror:

- Chairman Xi. What is going on?

Jing:

- Biyu? What the fuck are you doing in my office, you stupid cow? Call Dr Song Bao and tell him to get here immediately.

Biyu:

- But Dr Bao is not in Beijing today. Can I get someone else?

Jing:

- No! It has to be Dr Bao. Call him and get him to come here. Send a helicopter to his location and pick him up. Now leave!

Biyu did as Jing instructed and she rushed out of the room. "The bastards have poisoned me. I need to purge!" Jing thought and he crawled to the rubbish bin, put his fingers in his throat, and purged. After that, he passed out.

JING XI WOKE UP IN his private residence. Dr Bao and Jing's wife Lan Peng stood by his side. Lan sighed of relief:

- Oh, thank god you are awake. Dr Bao and I have been so worried about you.

Jing processed Lan's statement. He knew that it was a lie. His wife didn't give a shit about him, and he was certain that she had an affair with Chi Wang. Jing had been too busy scheming against the world and copulating with the beautiful Min Li, to verify the suspicion, but it was on his 'to-do' list.

Jing:

- Don't waste our time with this charade, Lan. Please leave the room. I need to speak to Dr Song Bao.

Lan Peng got up, and she left the room without saying a word. As she left the room, Jing turned towards Dr Song Bao and spoke:

- So, what happened to me? Did someone poison me?

Dr Bao shook his head and replied:

- I am afraid that your Hei Bai virus infection has activated at last. We might need to prepare for the worst. I have brought opioids to alleviate your pain.

Jing shook his head:

- I don't need to ease any pain. I am a fighter and I won't go down without a fight.

Dr Bao:

- As you wish, Chairman Xi. I will be nearby if you change your mind.

Jing:

- Dr Bao. Do you know if anyone else from the group has fallen ill yet?

Dr Bao:

- Not as far as I know. But I will find out for you.
- We don't have a cure against this virus, so what do you want me to do?

Jing:

- Stay in the background for now. I need to feel this virus myself. Only then can I understand it and learn from it.

Dr Bao:

- Understood. Just press the emergency button, and I will come. Best of luck, Chairman Xi.

As Dr Bao left the room, Jing started writhing in pain. His skin felt like he was on fire and he had to use his iron will to not scratch himself. He pulled himself together and he pulled off his shirt. Jing made his way to a mirror. He stared in horror as bark like streaks were spreading across his body. "I have to come up with something or I will die," Jing concluded.

Jing decided that he wouldn't call his doctor. That fool had suggested opioids to reduce the pain, but that wouldn't do anything against the symptoms. "Something I ate must have triggered the virus!" Jing thought. Could it be the Brazil Nuts? Jing decided that he would try an extreme measure to get out of his predicament. He would need to cleanse his body from toxins through sweating and shitting it all out. If he was wrong, he would die, but at least he would have died as a fighter. Jing pressed the emergency button and Song Bao rushed in.

Jing:

- Dr BAO. Bring me laxatives and ghost chilli at once.

Dr Bao stared at Jing's skin rash that was growing as he watched it. Dr Bao protested against the order:

- Are you insane? You cannot put your body under more stress. It will kill you.

Jing:

- So would your bloody opium. The white devils used opium against us during the 19th century. I will never succumb to such foreign influences. Now, do as I request. You might be my personal doctor, and the health minister, but I am the Chairman of CPOC!

Dr Bao:

- Understood, Heavenly Master.

Having said this, Song bowed and ran away to procure the supplies.

Dr Bao came back ten minutes later, and he handed Jing the laxatives and the ghost chilli. To his amazement, Jing skolled the bottle of laxatives and ate several of the super-strong chillies.

Jing:

- Please leave, I doubt that the coming hours will be pleasant.

Dr Bao did as Jing instructed and he hurried to leave Jing's private quarters. Jing rushed to the bathroom and braced himself for several unpleasant hours.

A FEW HOURS LATER, Jing emerged from the bathroom. He was severely dehydrated and covered in sickly stinking sweat. But it was worth it. The skin rash had reversed and it no longer pained him much. He pressed a button and Song Bao entered the room.

Dr Bao stared at Jing. Jing was pale, dressed in his underwear, and a thick layer of rancid sickly sweat covered his body. Jing smiled and spoke:

- I did it. I beat the Hei Bai virus. I would have died if I followed your advice.

Dr Bao:

- I don't understand. How could laxatives and chilli reverse your skin condition?

Jing:

- I thought about my day. The only thing I did differently today was that I ate a handful of Brazil nuts. Brazil nuts have a very high selenium content. Thus, selenium must be what is activating the Hei Bai virus. So, I drank heaps of laxatives and I ate a lot of chillies to excrete the selenium. It was hell, but at least it saved my life.

Dr Bao:

- This is amazing, Chairman Xi.

Jing:

- Yes. Get some medical staff here. I need a saline drip to recover. Also, send a large shipment of Brazil nuts to the Lop County concentration camps. We need to find out whether selenium is what triggers the virus.

Dr Bao:

- Understood, Chairman Xi. I will do your bidding.

After saying this, Dr Bao left the room while a medical team rushed in to attach Jing to a saline drip. Realising that he needed to recuperate, Jing didn't leave the bed for several days.

Chapter 11: Eileen receives a terrifying video. 1st of May 2021.

Eileen Lu was back in her home in Shanghai. She felt anxious knowing that Jing's AI monitored her. Fortunately, she had found a way to secure her laptop from government interference. At least she hoped that the government couldn't check her computer.

Eileen opened her email application. There was a message from Ming Shebao, a human rights activist, that she had defended in a recent court case. Ming's emails annoyed her. He was putting her at risk by sending her information. Knowing too much was dangerous, and although Eileen wanted to oppose the dictatorship, she also wanted to live.

Eileen couldn't contain her curiosity and she opened the video. It was terrifying. In the video, a dozen half-naked prisoners were screaming in agonizing pain. A bark-like rash was growing on their backs and spreading rapidly. At the end of the video clip, guards in hazmat suits came in and burned the prisoners alive with flamethrowers.

Eileen closed the video. She didn't know what to believe. The video didn't make sense and it was very likely to be fake. But why would Ming Shebao send her fake video? Perhaps Ming Shebao had swapped sides, and the Columnist Party wanted to discredit her movement. If she released a video that was later proven to be false, the Chinese dictatorship would use this as an argument against the civil rights movement.

Eileen closed Ming's email, and she was about to head out when another email hit her mailbox. It was from Jared Pond, the goofy Australian spy, who had failed to seduce her. What did he want? Eileen opened the email. It read:

"Hi, Eileen. I am visiting Shanghai at the moment. I recently resigned from RAKI, so you don't need to worry about what I do for work anymore. I bought some tickets for Moulin Rouge playing at the Pearl tomorrow night. Would you like to accompany me?"

Eileen shook her head. She couldn't think of a worse way to spend her time than going on a date with the boofhead that had hassled her twice in New York. The first time they met, he had spilled coffee on her, and during their second meeting he got into a fight and ended up in jail. What a loser!

But then an idea struck Eileen. What if she could give Jared a USB memory with the video that Ming had sent her, and ask Jared to post the video online? If the video was authentic, it was crucial that the world found out. If the video was fake, Jared would look like an idiot and Eileen's movement would not be discredited. Eileen sent the following reply:

"I would love to see the Moulin Rouge with you tomorrow. See you at the Pearl at 6 PM. Cheers Eileen."

Having sent her reply, Eileen put her phone in her handbag and she went to her workplace.

Chapter 12: Jing Xi Gets the Results from the Hei Bai Virus Testing. 2nd May 2021.

Jing Xi was sitting in his office when his health minister Dr Song Bao and Jing's security advisor Tzi Cheng entered his office. Dr Bao approached Jing, handed him a document and spoke:

- Chairman Xi. We have conducted the requested tests on the Uighurs at the Lop County Uighur concentration camp.

Jing:

- A bit slower than I had anticipated, but never mind. I needed to recuperate from my illness.

- What did you find?

Dr Bao:

- We found out that your hypothesis was correct. Selenium does trigger the virus.

Jing:

- Lucky, I didn't give in to my weakness and took the morphine. What exactly did you find?

Dr Bao:

- The virus becomes active and the carrier contagious at a daily intake of 100 micrograms of selenium. At 300 micrograms, serious symptoms appear. That's when a burning skin rash starts covering the back of the carrier. At a 500-micrograms intake of selenium, a person's entire body is covered by the skin rash. In this instance, the individual experiences prolonged excruciating pain that often kills the carrier.

Jing:

- Excellent. How much selenium is there in a Brazil nut?

Dr Bao:

- About 80 micrograms, Heavenly Master.

Jing:

- So, with this virus: Two nuts would make someone contagious; four nuts would make someone sick, and six nuts would kill someone.

Dr Bao:

- Well, individual tolerances to the virus can differ, but on average yes.

Jing thought back on his virus episode. He tried to recall how many nuts he had eaten before that damn cabinet meeting. He thought that the number was three, which meant that his 'cure' consisting of laxatives and chillies had not affected his outcome. Jing didn't want to admit that luck had saved his life, and instead, he asked:

- So, what about antibodies towards the virus. Can someone build tolerance through gradually increasing the selenium intake?

Dr Bao:

- Survivors do get antibodies while the virus remains dormant in the body. We haven't tested your hypothesis about increased tolerance towards the virus yet, Chairman Xi.

Jing:

- Well, then you should. We must learn about the virus before using it against our enemies. And see if you can figure out a way to make people eat selenium. I doubt that we can convince our enemies to eat heaps of Brazil nuts while we release the virus.

Dr Bao:

- Understood, Heavenly Master.

Jing:

- Dismissed, Dr Bao.

Hearing this, Dr Song Bao bowed to Jing and left the room. Jing turned towards Tzi Cheng.

- What do you have to report, Security Advisor Cheng?

Tzi Cheng:

- Someone leaked a video of our experiments to our enemy, Ming Shebao.

Jing:

- Really? I hope you have Ming Shebao in custody.

Tzi Cheng:

- Yes. We have him in a secure facility nearby.

Jing:

- Excellent. I am coming with you. We need to find out who he has told about this!

Tzi Cheng:

- You don't need to come, Chairman Xi.
- We can torture him and find out what he knows.

Jing smirked and replied:

- I know. But when it comes to Ming Shebao, I want to see him die.

Tzi Cheng:

- As you wish, Chairman Xi. I'll take you to our Ministry of State Security prison now.

After saying this, Jing and Tzi Cheng left the room. They travelled to the prison where Jing's infamous secret police kept and tortured their prisoners.

A WHILE LATER, JING and Tzi Cheng arrived at the interrogation room where they kept Ming Shebao. Jing studied Ming Shebao through a one-sided mirror. Ming Shebao was battered and bruised from the interrogation but worst was yet to come for him. Jing smiled. It would be a pure delight to watch his enemy die from the Hei Bai virus.
Jing looked at Tzi Cheng and said:

- Stay here, Tzi Cheng. Watch what happens if I give him these./

Jing grabbed a bag of Brazil nuts and entered the interrogation room where Ming Shebao was chained to a chair. Jing's appearance shocked Ming and he exclaimed.

- Chairman Jing Xi! I would never believe that you would come here yourself. Have you come to torture me?

Jing scoffed:

- Don't be silly. I have others to do that for me. I just wanted to talk to my long-term critic. I would be a fool if I didn't take the opportunity to learn from my enemies.

Ming Shebao:

- And what do I gain from allowing you to learn from me?

Jing:

- Ah, you're looking after yourself. I like it. But before we discuss business, let's chat a bit first, shall we? I brought some beer and some nuts.

Ming Shebao looked sceptically at Jing and replied:

- What is going on? First, you sent your men to torture me, and now you are offering me beer and nuts.

Jing:

- The torture wasn't my intention. Some of my men are overzealous and take their own initiatives. It's difficult to govern a nation of 1.4 billion souls after all.

Jing took one of the nuts and he chewed it slowly. According to Dr Bao, he would be infectious after two nuts. After that, he only needed to watch as the starving Ming Shebao ate the remaining nuts, and the Hei Bai virus took hold of his body.

Jing clapped his hands and shouted out:

- Tzi Cheng, bring in a TV. We are going to watch Beijing against Shanghai in the Chinese Super League.

Ming Shebao stared at Jing in surprise as Tzi Cheng rolled in a TV on a stand and then left the room.
Jing:

- Don't look so surprised, Ming. What better way to bridge our differences than watching soccer together? I like Beijing and you like Shanghai. Yet we are both linked together by our love for the sport.

Ming Shebao:

- Is this your metaphor for how we both love China despite our political differences?

Jing:

- Exactly. But for now, just eat the nuts and drink the beer. You must be starving.

Having said this, Jing picked up his second nut and smirked. He would feel an itch but Ming Shebao would feel like he was being burnt alive.
Ming Shebao relaxed and he started eating the nuts and drinking his beer. Jing smirked:

- Don't be shy. Have the rest of the nuts. I am saving myself for dinner.

Jing smiled as Ming devoured the remaining nuts, and then the two men sat silent for a while watching the game. In the halftime break, Jing turned to Ming, whose infection was taking hold of him:

- I know that you filmed our Lop County concentration camp. You must have been wondering what happened to those prisoners that we killed. You are about to experience it firsthand.

Ming:

- What? Have you poisoned me? How? We are eating the same nuts and drinking the same beer.

Jing:

- Not poisoned. Infected. I am carrying the same virus that those prisoners had. The selenium in those nuts activates the virus. The two nuts that I ate is enough to make me contagious. Six nuts plus the virus is enough to kill a man. You ate a dozen nuts. Let's just say you are in a for a world of pain. Muahaha.

Ming didn't reply. The pain was overwhelming him and he collapsed to the floor together with the chair he was chained to.
Ming:

- Ahh! It is so painful. Please make it stop. I'll do anything

Jing:

- That's what I want to hear. Who did you show the video from the Lop County camp? Why hasn't anyone tried uploading it on our Internet?

Ming:

- It's already on the Internet. I will expose your crimes against humanity, Jing.

Jing:

- No, it's not. Our AI would have found it.

- The most interesting part about the Hei Bai virus is that when the rash reaches its peak it feels like you are being burned alive. That's why our prisoners didn't even react when our guards with flamethrowers set them alight. As a matter of fact, being burnt alive was preferable to suffering the consequences of the virus.

Ming squirmed in pain on the floor. The pain was too much for him and he passed in and out of consciousness. Ming pleaded:

- Please make it stop. I'll do anything.

Jing clapped his hands and Tzi Cheng entered the room. Jing:

- Our prisoner is ready to confess his crimes. Shoot him and end his life on my signal.

Tzi Cheng nodded and he aimed his pistol towards Ming. Jing turned towards Ming:

- Give me a name and your pain will be over.

Ming wheezed:

- Eileen... Eileen Lu.

Tzi Cheng looked at Jing:

- Chairman Xi?

Jing shook his head:

- Don't waste a bullet, Tzi. This man is a goner. We have a job to do. Find someone to abduct Eileen Lu for me.

Tzi Cheng looked at Jing in bemusement:

- Abduct? You are the leader of China. Your word is the law. You can have the police arrest her.

Jing:

- No. Arresting her would complicate what I have in mind for her. Abducting her would suit me better. Muahaha.

Having said this, Jing left the room where Ming was dying an excruciating death. Jing smiled to himself. He couldn't wait to first have his way with Eileen and then send her off the same way that Ming Shebao died!

Chapter 13: Pierre Beaumont books a meeting with Jing Xi. 3rd May 2021.

Pierre Beaumont was studying the discussion between Jing Xi and Dr Song Bao, while he was sitting at his office in Switzerland. Having one of his proxy companies, Xeng Fao Technologies, which had won the contract to creating the 'Eternal Safeguard" AI that supervised China was valuable, as it gave Pierre a backdoor into the system. This allowed him to spy on important Chinese government meetings.

From listening to Jing, Pierre knew that he had struck gold. If he could acquire a controllable virus, he would rule the world. And once he ruled the world, he would develop the cure, to bereave Jing Xi of his weapon. But first, he needed to retrieve the virus, and Pierre had an idea. It was a risky idea, but fortune favoured the bold. He needed to meet with Jing Xi so that he could get hold of the virus and infect himself with the dormant but otherwise harmless virus, as it could only trigger its toxins when he has ingested selenium. If he had the virus in his bloodstream, he could extract it from his own blood. Then he would use the enhanced intelligence bestowed upon him by the Zetan monocle, to figure out how to use the virus.

Pierre picked up his phone and called Jing's office. Biyu Sang responded. Pierre felt irritated that he didn't have Jing's direct number. This was because Pierre hadn't been the CEO of the World Bank when they last met.

Pierre spoke:

- Hello. This is Pierre Beaumont from the World Bank. I need to speak to Chairman Jing Xi.

Biyu Sang:

- Chairman Xi is not in his office. Call back tomorrow.

Pierre frowned. He was one of the most influential men in the world and when he called someone, he expected them to receive his call. Pierre reprimanded Biyu:

- The CEO of the World Bank does not call back tomorrow. You better call your boss straight away to avoid dire consequences for your well-being.

Biyu:

- Okay. Please hold the line.

Biyu sighed. Pierre Beaumont sounded important so ignoring him was dangerous. But if he turned out to be unimportant, Jing would scold her for disturbing him! Biyu called Jing's private phone, and he sounded happier than usual.

Jing:

- Hi Biyu. What's on your mind?

Biyu:

- Pierre Beaumont from the World Bank called. He insisted on speaking with you straight away.

Jing:

- Very well. Forward his call to me.

The situation puzzled Jing. What could that French-speaking faggot Pierre Beaumont want? And who did he think he was, demanding to speak to Jing straight away? Jing was the most powerful man on the planet and Pierre was a money-grubbing poof. The phone connected and Pierre spoke:

- Chairman Xi. We need to meet tomorrow. My private jet will land at Beijing airport at 9 AM. I expect an appropriate reception.

Jing was about to scream obscenities and smash his phone but he stopped himself. Although Pierre was a rude peasant, and not as powerful as Jing, he was too powerful to mistreat. Instead, Jing replied:

- I am busy. But I expect to see you at the World Economic Forum in two weeks.

Pierre:

- Oh, that's a shame. I wanted to discuss the bank account of 'The Honey Dragon Inc.' at Credit Suisse. The Swiss Government is about to absorb its $5 billion balance.

Jing:

- You stay away from my money!

Pierre:

- Oh, so it is your money? We better meet up tomorrow and discuss the matter. I'll be landing at 9 AM at Beijing International Airport. Make sure that I am received well.

After saying this, Pierre hung up the phone. Jing, who was about to leave the secret prison was furious. Jing turned to Tzi Cheng and exclaimed.

- Give me your pistol. I need to blow off some steam.

Tzi handed Jing his pistol, and Jing rushed into the cell where Ming Shebao was dying from the Hei Bai virus.
Jing:

- Fuck you, Dog!

After screaming this, he shot Ming Shebao with 15 bullets emptying the magazine of the gun!

Chapter 14: A Disrupted Date. 3rd May 2021.

Eileen Lu was studying herself in one of the grand mirrors at the Pearl in Shanghai. She had agreed to meet up with Jared Pond. To wrap him around her finger, she had dressed according to his preferences. The velvet red ballroom dress made Eileen stand out like a beacon in the crowd. Eileen smiled. Eileen liked to look beautiful, but she preferred when people measured her on her intellectual attributes.

Eileen felt bemused by the fact that she had agreed to meet with Jared. He was a buffoon, who believed himself to be every woman's dream. But she needed an ally. She needed someone that could post the video from the Uighur concentration camps online, without drawing attention to her. Jared was that someone.

Eileen saw Jared approaching. He was casually dressed, like she had been when they met at the cocktail bar in New York. Eileen smiled. It seemed like they had second-guessed each other.

Eileen walked up to Jared and seduced:

- Hi Jared. You look great today. Are you having a casual evening?

Jared:

- Well. I didn't know that you'd look so stunning today. I thought that we could meet up as friends.

Eileen teased:

- So, are friends what we are?

Jared:

- Well, unless starstruck lovers is an option?

Eileen:

- It might be.

- Let's head to the bar. I would love you to educate me on cocktails and champagnes!

Jared:

- People have told me that I am a great teacher.

Eileen:

- Of that, I am certain

After saying this, Eileen took Jared's hand as she allowed him to lead her to the bar section of the venue.

They got seated at a table, and the waiter delivered their drinks, a mojito for Eileen and a whisky sour for Jared. Eileen smiled at Jared:

- So, what brings you to Shanghai, Jared?

Jared:

- Isn't the performance and your lovely company good enough reasons?

Eileen:

- Yes. But you came here yesterday. Before I had accepted to meet you.

Jared:

- Yesterday, I was in Macao skimming some rich Chinese business-men in poker.

- Would you like another drink?

Eileen:

- Yeah, I'll have what you are having.

Jared:

- Excellent choice, Eileen.

As Jared walked up to the bar, Eileen felt tipsy. She wasn't a big drinker, so the cocktail had got her gears moving. She needed to get Jared away from the crowds so that she could experience him on her own. Eileen felt silly. Until now she hadn't even liked Jared, and yet she felt attracted to him? Perhaps it was a physical need that she needed to fulfil, to get away from all the stress and paranoia that the concentration camp video had caused her.

Jared returned with their cocktails and they got involved in some more idle chatter until a bell rang.

Jared:

- The show is about to begin.

Eileen was getting intoxicated and she slurred:

- How about we head straight to your hotel room?

Jared smiled and teased:

- Business or pleasure?

Eileen:

- I need to show you something. After that, I am very much up for pleasure.

Jared:

- Very well. Come with me, and I'll teach you how to spend a full
night of passion.

EILEEN WAS RIDING JARED with wild enthusiasm when she realised that
she hadn't told him about the virus testing video. She paused for a second. She
hadn't had sex since the separation from her fiancée a year earlier. Part of her
would love to have that fourth consecutive orgasm, but she needed to focus on
her duty to her country.

Jared smiled at Eileen and teased:

- Are you getting tired already? It's only been twenty minutes.

Eileen was collecting herself from the exhilarating experience. She was
about to reply when the door opened and two shady Chinese men ran in.

One of the men rushed to Eileen and punched her in the gut, knocking her
to the ground. The combination of shock, physical trauma and alcohol knocked
Eileen out.

"I should not have taken all that Viagra. This is awkward." Jared thought.

Jared got up from the bed. He wore no clothes, and he was sporting an erection. This was his first fight for survival while being naked, and hopefully, there
wouldn't be many too follow.

One of the attackers kicked Jared on the balls and was amazed as Jared
hardly flinched. Being a prominent womanizer, Jared had developed a tolerance
to ball-busting kicks, and it would take more than that to put him down. Jared
responded in kind, and the first attacker was gasping for air on the ground, with
his prospect of future fatherhood diminished.

"Don't come uninvited!" Jared exclaimed. Jared rushed over to the second
attacker, punched him in the face, and then dropped a TV over him. After this,
Jared ran back to the first attacker and knocked him out with a knee to the face.

Jared put on his pants, and he checked on Eileen.

Eileen:

- Uh. What happened?

Jared:

- Some intruders decided to interrupt our lovely evening. But we shouldn't let them. Let's head over to your place and continue from where we were.

Eileen:

- So, you want to have more sex after men attacked us?

Jared:

- What better way to relieve stress?

Eileen:

- Okay. I have booked a cab to my place.
- Let's get out of here.

Having said this, Eileen and Jared hurried to grab their stuff, and they left the room before their attackers woke up.

THE NEXT MORNING, EILEEN woke up with a terrible headache. She had drunk too much alcohol and getting assaulted by assassins didn't help. Furthermore, her marathon session with the tireless Jared Pond had dehydrated her. She made her way to the kettle and boiled some tea. She diluted the hot tea with tap water so that she could drink it quickly. After a few cups, she remembered the USB with the video. She tapped Jared on the shoulder and he woke up with a smile:

- Good morning, sunshine. Are you ready for another session?

Eileen shook her head and replied:

- As lovely as that would be, we agreed on business and pleasure. And we haven't dealt with the business part yet.

Jared sighed:

- I see. What is it that you want to discuss?

Eileen opened her laptop and showed Jared the video from the Uighur concentration camp. Jared looked at the video sceptically for a while and replied:

- Where did you get this video from?

Eileen:

- One of my former clients sent it to me. I cannot disclose who it was.

Jared:

- Was it Ming Shebao?

Eileen gave Jared a worried look and held her tongue.
Jared:

- Don't worry, Eileen. I am a former spy. This is what I do.

- Ming Shebao doesn't have the best reputation overseas, due to making erroneous claims in the past. But I am sure that you know about this already?

Eileen nodded.
Jared:

- So, I take it that you want me to publish these claims? In that case, I would need to verify them with RAKI first.

Eileen:

- But didn't you quit?

Jared:

- Yes, but this video is explosive stuff. I need to verify it before I release it on the Internet. I am not a conspiracy theorist that releases anything I get hold of.

Eileen:

- I understand. Don't take too long. People are suffering and we cannot know what more crimes Jing Xi is planning against humanity.

Jared:

- Agreed.

- Did you recognise the men that attacked us last night? I think you were the one who got us in trouble this time!

Eileen shook her head and replied:

- Well, they didn't come here, so it must have been you.

Jared:

- Just my luck. We should leave China to be safe.

Eileen shook her head and replied:

- You should leave, but I am not going anywhere. I need to congregate with our civil liberties movement and celebrate the second Qingming festival in Xuwan.

Jared:

- Isn't the Qingming festival in April?

Eileen:

- You know a lot about China, Jared.

- The second Qingming festival is not a real event. We are gathering to honour the ones who fell in the last stand against tyranny in 1989. We are not allowed to commemorate those heroes, so we created the second Qingming festival instead.

Jared:

- Very well. I better head back to Australia. It would be lovely if you decided to visit me there, after your celebration.

Eileen felt sorrow gripping her mind. She would love to move to Australia and leave this mess behind her. But she couldn't let Jing Xi go unchecked. If she did, his tyranny would spread, and he would subjugate the whole world. Eileen:

- Thank you, Jared. I hope to see you soon. Make sure to spread my video.

Jared nodded, kissed Eileen goodbye, took a taxi to the airport and boarded the next flight back to Australia.

Chapter 15: A Frosty Meeting. 4th May 2021.

Pierre Beaumont exited his limousine outside the presidential palace of China. He wasn't particularly impressed. While China had experienced impressive economic development, it was still a polluted shithole. Nothing compared to Switzerland, which had great cities and beautiful mountains just a short drive away!

Pierre reminded himself of his plan. He had added a grain of selenium hydride to a jar of Elvish honey. It was a dangerous plan. Pierre needed to get Jing Xi to ingest enough selenium to become infectious, but not so much so that he got the symptoms. Making Jing eat the right amount of selenium added honey to get the right level was almost impossible. Pierre sighed. He would have to settle for making Jing eat Brazil nuts. It was a risky and conspicuous plan, but it was the only way to get the dosage right.

Pierre reached the reception area of the presidential palace, where an attendant told him to stay and wait. Pierre looked at his luxurious Swiss watch. He would get upset if Jing kept him waiting. Pierre was certain that Jing would keep him waiting. They didn't like each other, and for now, Jing was the more powerful of the two, although that was about to change. Pierre smiled when he thought about how he would reform the world and enrichen himself.

JING XI FELT JITTERY and frustrated. The men he had sent to kidnap Eileen Lu, had failed miserably and had ended up in the hospital. Eileen's contact, the Australian agent Jared Pond, had evaded the country, no doubt carrying a copy of the virus testing video. Jing thought of his next step. It would be easy for him to have Eileen arrested and killed, but he desired her body, which he couldn't have if she was officially arrested. Jing had evil thoughts about Eileen. Raping her and then letting the Hei Bai virus kill her would be a great pleasure. But first, he needed to deal with Jared Pond. Jing walked over to Tzi Cheng and whispered:

- Contact our Australian friends and make sure that Jared Pond doesn't release the virus testing video on the Internet.

Tzi Cheng nodded and rushed away to make the arrangements.
One of the palace attendants approached Jing:

- Chairman Xi. Pierre Beaumont has arrived and he is waiting for you in the sun dragon room.

Jing:

- Good. I'll be there shortly.

Jing reflected over his options. On the one hand, he wanted Pierre to wait for him. Pierre was a lowly banker, and as such he should wait for the emperor. But on the other hand, Jing had nothing else to do, so wasting his own time to make Pierre wait for him was irrational. Jing sighed and realised that he was better off meeting Pierre straight away. That way he would get this issue dealt with.

PIERRE FAKED A SMILE as Jing greeted him. This would be difficult, but he had to overcome the difficulties.
Pierre:

- Thank you for seeing me on such a short notice, Chairman Xi.

Jing:

- Extraordinary circumstances require extraordinary measures. How can I resolve this problem with my Credit Suisse account?

Pierre:

- As the CEO of the World Bank, I can call them and make them re-activate the account.

- But first, let's exchange gifts. I brought you this jar of honey and these Brazil nuts. I have heard that nuts dipped in honey is a delicacy.

Having said this, Pierre froze for a second. What if the combination of the contaminated honey and the brazil nuts would cause a full virus outbreak in Jing's body? Pierre shook off the thought, he was here now, and he could only roll with it.

Jing looked at Pierre for a while and then he dipped one of the brazil nuts in the honey and smiled:

- You are right, Pierre. Nuts and honey are a great combination.

Pierre:

- Yes of course. Let's have one more but without the honey flavour. They have a great and unique flavour, don't they?

Jing picked up another nut, hesitated for a while, ate the nut, and replied:

- Yes. They are a favourite of mine. But we can't have more than this, we need to save ourselves for morning tea.

After saying this, Jing pointed in the direction of a set table. He handed his attendant the nuts and honey and they walked to the table.

Jing:

- Traditional Chinese breakfast.

Pierre looked at the food and taunted:

- Oh, I was hoping for bat soup. Nothing beats the emergence of another virus.

Jing's gaze blackened but he contained his anger. Jing:

- So, why did you insist on meeting me today?

Pierre:

- I wanted to discuss some changes to your Silk and Belt Road project. It is clashing with our Human Rights Project in Almaty, Kazakhstan.

Jing:

- Since when does the World Bank care about human rights?

Pierre:

- I don't care about human rights per se, but they are a great tax write off and good for the reputation of the bank.

Jing:

- Bah. When China first became wealthy, we thought that we needed to pretend to care. But we soon realised that no-one gives a shit about human rights, as long as the money flows.

Pierre:

- Interesting approach, but let's discuss how we can synchronize our projects in Almaty. The world will be a better place if we coordinate our efforts.

Jing nodded and they discussed their business interests in Almaty for half an hour. After half an hour, Jing was getting itchy. He thought about whether he had inadvertently activated the Hei Bai virus. It couldn't be the case. He had antibodies to the virus in his body now, so his selenium tolerance should have gone up. He rushed back to his office and he told Biyu to summon Dr Bao.

DR SONG BAO:

- Your blood test shows that you must have ingested over 300 micrograms of selenium. Lucky that you already had some tolerance to the Hei Bai Virus.

Jing:

- How is that possible? Those nuts should have contained less than half of that.

Dr Song Bao:

- Perhaps there was something special with the nuts. Do you still have the bag?

Jing:

- No, I gave it to one of the attendants, Mie Yung. I told her to throw it away.

Dr Song Bao:

- Well, I better find her and retrieve the contents of that bag. You stay here and recover. The virus is receding already and your excess selenium should be depleted in a couple of hours.

Jing nodded. While he hated hiding away in his office, he could not show himself in public until his terrifying skin rash had disappeared.

PIERRE BEAUMONT WAS back in his mansion in Switzerland, which had a small research lab in the basement. He had extracted some of his blood, and his plan had worked. There were traces of dormant Hei Bai virus in his blood, which he had received from the encounter with Jing Xi. Pierre Beaumont studied the virus in a microscope. He had taken a huge risk, travelling to China and getting himself infected by Jing Xi. But it would be worth it. He had the virus dormant in his blood stream and with a controllable virus in his hand, he could control the world markets and the world economy. Once Pierre had set his plan in motion, the future was his.

Chapter 16: Greg Steel arrests Jared Pond at Sydney Airport. 5th May 2021.

Jared was sitting in the business class of the Qantas Flight 130 from Shanghai headed to Sydney. He looked at the virus testing video from the Uighur concentration camp. It was full of terrifying images and Jared couldn't get over the hunch that it could be real. But he needed to verify the content with his former colleagues at RAKI before he spread it. Tensions were still large in the world after the Coronavirus plandemic, and more villainy from China could cause outright war. Thus, Jared needed to be on the safe side before acting.

A thought struck Jared. What if Greg Steel would confiscate and delete the videos? There was a possibility, particularly if Scurry Morrissett prioritised licking Jing Xi's boots over doing what was right. Jared came up with the solution. He would upload the video on a lot of official and secret platforms on the Internet. Then he would set the video to publish in 14 days unless he cancelled it. This way, he had plenty of time to determine whether the video was fake or real, and the Australian government couldn't silence him to please China.

Having decided on a course of action, Jared spent the flight back to Sydney, implementing his plan. Once he had finished, he formatted his computer and mobile phone to stop his colleagues from tracking his steps. He leaned back into his seat, and he fell asleep.

WHEN JARED ARRIVED in Sydney, Greg Steel and a host of federal police officers were waiting for him at the gate. Greg approached him:

- What were you doing in China, Jared? Our Chinese friends have sent a warrant for your arrest.

Jared:

- I am no longer working for the RAKI, so it's none of your business. But I had a rendezvous with the beautiful Eileen Lu.

Greg:

- Yes. But why did you assault two security guards at the Shangrila Hotel in Shanghai?

Jared:

- When people storm into my room in the middle of the night, I would classify any violence against them as self-defence.

Greg:

- Well, the Chinese doesn't. They have requested that we send you back. But first, we need to interrogate you to find out the truth. Please come with us.

Jared:

- Sure. But please analyse this critical piece of evidence that I found. I got this video from Ming Shebao and it shows how the Chinese government is testing a new virus on prisoners.

Greg:

- Thank you, Jared. I will look into this.
- Officers, please bring Jared to the RAKI holding facility in Pyrmont.

Having said this, Greg seized Jared's USB memory, phone, and laptop. After this, he headed back to his office to decide his course of action.

A FEW HOURS LATER, Greg Steel was talking to Jing Xi over the phone
Greg:

- It's a great honour to speak to you, Chairman Xi.

Jing:

- Spare the pleasantries. Tzi Cheng told me that you had some alarming news.

Greg:

- Yes. Jared Pond carried an incriminating video. It shows how the Chinese government is testing a deadly pathogen on prisoners.

Jing:

- Jared Pond is a criminal who colluded with the fraudster Ming Shebao and assaulted security guards.

Greg:

- And what about the video?

Jing:

- The video isn't real and the Hei Bai virus doesn't exist.

Greg:

- Why do you have a name for it, if it doesn't exist?

Jing:

- Bah. Our AI analyses all the communications of Chinese citizens. We know what the enemies of the nation are discussing amongst themselves.

Greg:

- Understood. There is one more problem. Jared had formatted his phone and his computer. I believe that he anticipated arrest and uploaded the videos all over the Internet.

Jing:

- That would be unfortunate. We need to access his computer and phone. Our AI can restore everything that Jared is trying to hide. Also, please send our men a log of all the WIFI usage from QF130.

Greg:

- Understood. What are we going to do with Jared?

Jing:

- You need to bring him to me.

Greg:

- That would be difficult. Australia is not extraditing prisoners to China. Should I ask Scurry Morrissett for an exception?

Jing:

- No. Find a way to do it covertly. There will be a $20 million reward for your troubles.

Greg:

- Understood, Chairman Xi. I will contact Tzi Cheng about our arrangements.

Jing:

- Great. Discuss all further arrangements with Tzi Cheng. Dismissed, Colonel Steel.

After finishing the conversation with Jing, Greg leaned back into his chair and rubbed his hands. After serving his country for many years, it was finally time to serve himself!

Chapter 17: Pierre Beaumont Plans for a Controlled Virus Outbreak. 6th May 2021.

Pierre Beaumont was at home in his mansion overlooking Lake Geneva in Switzerland. He put through an order for 20 kilograms of selenium hydride. He sent it to the New York office of Jing Xi's shelf company "The Honey Dragon Inc.". While Pierre had shelf companies of his own, it was better if the blame for the outbreak fell on China when it was all over. Pierre suspected that Jing Xi planned to strike during the World Leader Summit at the United Nations Headquarters in New York. Jing seemed to be planning for a minor outbreak at the United Nations to cover up the real attack on the Civil Rights movement in Xuwan. Pierre, however, had another goal. If he could wipe out the majority of the world leaders, the global markets would collapse. Predicting the crash, he could short every share of the global economy, using the World Banks wealth as collateral. Once the dust had settled, Pierre would be the wealthiest person on the planet.

Vladimir Kravchenko entered Pierre's residence. Pierre studied the thuggish Russian who was both Pierre's occasional lover as well as Pierre's most accomplished assassin. Pierre found Vladimir both attractive and terrifying at the same time. Aided by the same alien technology as Pierre, Vladimir had supersenses that made him the most accomplished covert operative in the world. Pierre feared Vladimir's lust to murder and torture people. While Pierre didn't mind if people died as long as he benefitted, he saw no value in needless suffering. Vladimir was different. He didn't care about money, but nothing meant more to him than the opportunity to maim and torture people to fulfil his sadistic needs.

Vladimir:

- You summoned me, Pierre. Is this about business or pleasure?

Pierre:

- Are they not one and the same?

Vladimir nodded, Pierre gave him a USB memory and spoke:

- I summoned you about business. I have ordered 20 kilograms of selenium hydride to an address in New York. I need you to collect the selenium and contaminate a water processing plant. This plant provides the United Nations headquarters with drinking water. I plan to attack the UN summit on the 14th of May to cause mass panic and crash the markets to enrichen myself.

Vladimir focused for a while as the monocle gave him an estimate of casualties such an attack would cause. Eventually, he spoke:

- What's the point of that? Selenium is only dangerous if you ingest more than 5 milligrams a day. The delegates would have to drink 10 litres of water for that to happen.

Pierre smiled and replied:

- Good thinking, Vladimir. But I am not aiming to kill anyone via selenium poisoning.

Vladimir looked at Pierre in confusion and replied:

- So, what is the point of this then?

Pierre:

- Behold the Hei Bai virus, Muahaha.

Pierre showed Vladimir a model of the Hei Bai virus. Vladimir shook his head and replied:

- Who cares? Why are you showing me this virus, Pierre?

Pierre smirked and turned on the video of the Hei Bai virus testing in the Uighur concentration camp in China. Vladimir studied the video and marvelled at the pain and the suffering of the prisoners. He almost orgasmed when he saw how the guards torched the prisoners with their flamethrowers.
Pierre:

- That is the Hei Bai virus, Vladimir. A high dosage of selenium in the body activates the virus. I estimate that everyone who drinks more than one litre of contaminated water will get serious symptoms and die at the meeting.

Vladimir:

- Excellent. But some of them will survive?

Pierre:

- Viruses don't kill everyone infected. It will look more natural if there are survivors. Besides I am only after the market collapse to en-richen myself.

Vladimir:

- I like your plan. Let's fuck!

Pierre shook his head and replied:

- We'll only fuck after you have completed the mission. But don't worry. I have organised a new victim for you. Aleksei has kidnapped another street urchin, a Syrian refugee. That will have to suffice for now.

- I'll meet you in New York on the 14th of May.

Vladimir licked his lips and replied:

- Ah. I love the young Syrian refugees. I'll enjoy my evening and then I'll travel to New York to prepare for the attack.

Pierre:

- Great. Enjoy your night.

After hearing this, Vladimir walked up to Pierre's computer and pressed a few commands. Pierre shouted:

- Stay away from my computer, Vladimir. We are close but not that close!

Vladimir smiled maliciously and replied:

- Of course, Pierre. I will follow your command.

Having said this, Vladimir left Pierre's residence while whistling a joyful tune.

Chapter 18: Greg Steel abducts Jared Pond and ships him off to China. 7th May 2021.

Jared Pond was staring at the wall of his prison cell. He didn't like the fact that Greg had locked him up in a secret RAKI facility instead of in a normal jail cell. Something was amiss and he wondered what he would do. He wouldn't tell anyone which websites he had posted the video on. The world needed to know and the video was real, there could not be any other explanation to his imprisonment. But was Jared's imprisonment Greg's idea, or was Scurry Morrissett behind it all?

"Speaking of the devil!" Jared thought when Greg Steel and Michael Walker entered the cell. Greg spoke:

- Good news, Jared. You are free to go. Scurry doesn't want to hand you over to the Chinese government.

Jared:

- What about the video? Did you analyse it yet?

Greg:

- That is a question of national security that I will not disclose to civilians.

- Follow me. I'll escort you out.

Jared sighed of relief. Once he was out of this mess, he would hide in the outback for a while, staying out of sight from Chinese agents. It had been a while since Jared was camping by himself in the wilderness. There was something cleansing about enjoying the clear night sky of the Australian outback. Jared's thoughts didn't get much further than that. He felt a pinprick in his neck when Michael injected him with a sedative. Jared tried to stand up and fight, but he didn't get far and he collapsed unconscious to the floor.

WHEN JARED WOKE UP, he was on a private jet. He was bound to a chair and surrounded by four Chinese agents and Greg Steel.

Jared felt dizzy and he mumbled:

- Greg? What is going on?

Greg taunted Jared:

- Isn't that obvious? I am selling you to the Chinese Ministry of State Security.

Jared:

- Why? I thought that we were friends?

Greg:

- Friends? You were my disrespectful subordinate. I accepted your philandering and gambling as you delivered results.

- But Jing offered me something better. USD 20 million for delivering you to China.

Jared:

- He is never going to pay you! You are being duped.

Greg:

- He has already paid me. Besides we are refuelling the plane in Singapore. I'll get off there.

Jared:

- You'll never get away with this!

Greg:

- Oh, I am sure that feckless Scurry will fire me for this. But what else can he do? Issue an international arrest warrant and cause a diplomatic crisis with China? You don't think he cares that much about your well-being, do you?

Jared:

- Fuck you, Greg. You'll pay for your crimes. I'll come after you myself.

Greg:

- No, you won't.

Having said this, Greg electrocuted Jared with a Taser. Then he gagged Jared to avoid listening to Jared's ranting. The plane landed and Greg got off. Jared could hear that the employees outside was refuelling the plane. He tried to scream but he was gagged so it was to no avail. "Oh, if I only had one of those Bond gadgets," Jared thought, but he didn't. One of the Chinese agents injected some more sedatives into Jared's body, and he fell unconscious.

Chapter 19: Tzi Cheng interrogates Jared Pond. 8th May 2021.

Jared was sitting in a gloomy interrogation room in a Chinese Ministry of State Security facility in Beijing. He had been in trouble before but this was it. Being locked up in the Chinese dictatorship's facilities was a death sentence. Jared knew that the only reason he was alive, was so they could find out where he had posted the virus testing video. Jared damned Greg for betraying him and the world to Jing's tyranny.

The door opened and Tzi Cheng entered the room. He was a muscular and stout man with a dangerous appearance. A large scar ran along the left side of his face. Without a word, he walked up to Jared and punched him in the face. Jared dropped to the ground and two soldiers ran in to tilt the chair that bound Jared, to an upright position.

Tzi Cheng:

- Welcome to China, foreign scum!

Jared:

- Thank you. Can you tickle my chin again? I think I got a mosquito bite there.

Tzi Cheng:

- There are better ways for me to inflict pain on you, than punching you. As a matter of fact, I have developed a whole array of torture methods under Jing's glorious leadership.

Jared:

- Well, I must be pretty important if Jing's top security advisor, Tzi Cheng, comes down to torture me.

Tzi Cheng:

- You have done your research, Mr Pond.

- You are only a speck of dust to the Chinese government. But the fake video that you have posted online is dangerous and we must take it down before it spreads.

Jared:

- How can a fake video threaten your authority? The real threat for you is that the video is real and you don't want evidence against you when you release the virus.

Tzi Cheng:

- Very well. The video is real. But you are not getting out of here alive in any case.

Jared:

- Good to have cleared that out. So, why would I help you then?

Tzi Cheng:

- Because I have a vast array of torture methods that I would like to test on you. Let's start with electricity.

Having said this, Tzi Cheng electrocuted Jared with a cattle rod, multiple times, while he laughed in delight.

A FEW HOURS LATER, Tzi Cheng reported his progress at Jing's office.
Jing:

- So, what have you found out?

Tzi Cheng:

- Our torture of Jared hasn't worked so far. But we found all the sites that he posted the video on through studying the Wi-Fi usage on his flight.

Jing:

- So, did you take them down?

Tzi Cheng:

- We got most of the major sites to take them down. The threat of economic sanctions from China was enough to make most of the major video sites bending over backwards. Jared set the videos to release on the 19th of May.

Jing:

- This is excellent. That gives us ample time to exert pressure on all the sites to have the video removed. It also explains why our AI hasn't detected and warned us about the video.

- Why do you reckon Jared set the videos to release on the 19th?

Tzi Cheng:

- I reckon that he trusted Greg enough to wait for his input, but he still made copies of the video as an insurance policy.

Jing:

- You might be right. Don't worry about Jared for now. Leave him in a cell and don't kill him.

Tzi Cheng:

- Why do you want to keep him alive?

Jing:

- Because I will blame him, Eileen Lu, and the civil rights movement for the outbreak that will take place in Xuwan next week. I can't use him as a scapegoat if I kill him now, can I?

Tzi Cheng:

- So, do you want me to release him?

Jing shook his head:

- No. Wait until the 15th of May. Then release him in Xuwan and entice him to find Eileen Lu. It's time to crush the civil liberties movement, once and for all.

After saying this Jing feasted on a jar of expensive honey and laughed maliciously for an extended period of time.

Chapter 20: Pierre Gets a Copy of the Virus Testing Video. 8th May 2021.

Pierre woke up as his monocle was beeping. He had set the Zetan Monocle and it's intuitive advanced AI to wake him up if there were any important developments in the world. Pierre smiled when he saw the video with the conversation between Jing and Tzi Cheng. If he could acquire the virus testing video, he would have ample evidence to frame the Chinese government. If he played his cards right, he could crush China and increase his power. It was the opportunity of a lifetime for Pierre.

Pierre downloaded the list of websites that had refused to take down the virus video. He started contacting the website administrators. After a few hours, Pierre reached King Mwanza from a Nigeran herbal medicine website.

King:

- Hey, who is this?

Pierre:

- This is Chi Wong. I am interested in a video of yours.

King:

- Are you talking about that Chinese video? I am not taking it down unless you pay me a lot. That video could make me a fortune from selling herbal remedies to the disease in the video. I am already scaling up production.

Pierre:

- How can you have a treatment when you don't even have a sample of the virus?

King:

- I don't need one. I operate on faith. My followers believe in my herbal remedies. Faith trumps science.

Pierre:

- And money trumps both.
- I have an offer for you.

King:

- I am not removing that video.

Pierre:

- I don't expect you to. As a matter of fact, I want a copy of the video sent to me. I am willing to pay you USD 10 million for the video.

King:

- Who are you?

Pierre:

- A friend wanting to do the right thing. So, do we have a deal?

King:

- You need to pay me upfront, man.

Pierre:

- That can be organised.

- I'll send you the money on an anonymous Swiss bank account. I expect you to transfer me the video, to avoid 'unfortunate' accidents from happening.

King:

- You got it, man. I will send you the file as soon as you have paid me. You know how to reach me.

Having said this, King Mwanza hung up the phone. Pierre logged in to Credit Suisse and paid Mwanza with Jing's hidden bank account. Pierre smirked. Jing was too afraid of losing his hidden bank account to ask the real question, how Pierre knew about the account in the first place!

A few minutes later, Pierre received the virus testing video. After securing the video Pierre instructed the monocle to upload the video everywhere under 100's of different user names. He would release the video on 16th of May. Then Pierre took off the monocle, put it close to the Wi-fi router and went to sleep. Pierre dreamt about his rise to become the true puppet master of the world.

Chapter 21: Jing Xi Travels to New York. 10th May 2021.

Jing Xi boarded the Chinese government plane that would take him to the United Nations summit in New York on the 12th of May. Everything was going according to plan. Jing would cause a minor outbreak at the United Nations summit to divert media attention from the Xuwan outbreak. The Chinese civil rights movement was congregating in Xuwan, and what better way to get rid of them than causing a massive outbreak? Jing would then lock down the city and have his secret police murdering everyone that opposed him. In the aftermath, Jing would claim that the Hei Bai virus caused their deaths.

To create the Xuwan outbreak, Jing had transferred infected Uighur prisoners to the city. Furthermore, he had ordered Tzi Cheng to contaminate the water supply with large amounts of selenium hydride. The selenium would activate the dormant Hei Bai virus and make millions sick within a matter of days. Thousands would die from the virus, but many more would die from the purges that Jing would put through during the lockdown. Likewise, Jing would cause minor outbreaks in other cities, to motivate lockdowns there. In the end, everyone that the AI had identified as his opponents, 1.2 million people, would be wiped off the face of the Earth. After the genocide, the Columnist Party of China would reign supreme and people would have to deify Jing.

When it came to the summit in New York, Jing would pick a more careful approach. He had ordered the caterer, which he owned, to supply Brazil nuts at most of the conference tables. Some people would undoubtedly get sick, which would steal all the media attention. But most delegates wouldn't touch the nuts and wouldn't get sick. Furthermore, Jing had ordered the caterer to serve the important delegates other snacks to avoid triggering the virus.

Jing called his right-hand-man Tzi Cheng:

- Is everything ready?

Tzi Cheng:

- Yes. We have transferred Jared and the infected Uighurs to Xuwan.
We will release them and contaminate the water supply in two days.

Jing:

- Excellent. Have you organised the minor outbreaks and the lockdowns of our other major cities?

Tzi Cheng:

- Yes. We are ready to move in and seize all the enemies of China during this glorious time of our history.

- It's a shame that you cannot lead us through the great purge.

Jing:

- Yes. But I have to visit the United Nations. I have to get infected
myself to prove that I am innocent and that the enemies of China are
behind this.

Tzi Cheng:

- Yes. I know. Best of luck, Chairman Xi.

Jing:

- For China and the rise of the dragon! Dismissed, Tzi.

After saying this, Jing hung up the phone. He felt uncomfortable knowing
that he would have to get sick with the Hei Bai Virus to create an alibi for him-

self. But it was a risk that he was willing to take. When it came to strengthening the power of himself and his party, no risk was too high.

"Bring me some honey liqueur, slave." Jing shouted to Biyu, and he leaned back in his chair full of joy, as the sweet drops satisfied his taste buds, and the alcohol calmed his senses.

Chapter 22: Pierre Beaumont Travels to New York. 11th May 2021.

"I would like a glass of Penfolds Grange Shiraz 2015." Pierre said with a smug voice. Pierre sat on board his private jet, headed from Geneva to New York and he felt amazing. He sipped the wine. It didn't taste as good as the 2012 vintage despite costing $200 more. Regardless of this temporary setback, Pierre felt excited. He would soon become the richest man on the planet and he would never need to worry about money again.

Pierre had considered whether he needed to travel to New York at all. He could do all the trading from the safety of his home in Geneva. He had decided that his presence in New York was advantageous. Pierre was a control freak, and he couldn't relinquish control of the entire operation to Vladimir. He needed to be there himself. Pierre had invested billions in CFD-s and shorting the market. He had used the World Bank's money as a security for all the anonymous letterbox companies that he had set up. If the outbreak didn't happen, he would have lost most of the money that he had invested, and the entire world would come after him. Even with his heightened intelligence, Pierre would be in serious trouble under such a scenario.

Struck by his fear of failure, Pierre lashed out at his servant:

- 2015 is not a good vintage. Bring me a glass of 2012 vintage.

Servant:

- I am sorry, sir. We didn't bring any 2012 vintage. Can I suggest 2014?

Pierre:

- 2014? I'd rather drink this cat piss that you served me. Go away.

The servant rushed off without a word.

Pierre felt remorseful. While he didn't mind the prospect of murdering thousands to enrichen himself, he shouldn't treat his staff like they were dogs. Such was the behaviour of that brute and simple idiot Jing Xi, but Pierre was a superior human. A superior human didn't allow minor setbacks to change his behaviour to that of a lesser animal.

Pierre took out a few 100-swiss-francs banknotes and he got up from his seat. He walked over to his servant and spoke:

- I am sorry, Michelle. Your transgression didn't warrant such a brutish behaviour from me. Here is a token of appreciation. Buy your daughter Eva a present from me.

Michelle:

- Thank you, Pierre. That is very generous of you.

Pierre:

- But don't allow complacency. We will return to Geneva in two days, and I need you to get me the 2012 vintage by then. Money is, as always, not an issue.

Michelle:

- Thank you, Pierre. I will do everything that I can, to satisfy your request.

Pierre nodded and didn't reply. A minor dilemma struck him. He didn't want his servant to die, but he worried that he would expose himself if he warned Michelle. He shrugged off the notion and decided that he could save his servant while maintaining his alibi at the same time.

Pierre:

- Just a heads up. I have heard that New York tap water is unsafe to drink. Only drink bottled water from our Swiss Alps while you are there. Take enough bottled water from the plane to last for two days.

Michelle:

- Thank you, Pierre. I will.

After warning Michelle, Pierre felt a bit worried. What if warning Michelle would affect his plan? Pierre shrugged off the notion. A lot of people had warranted and unwarranted objections towards drinking tap water. As long as he didn't tell Michelle why the tap water was dangerous to drink, his statement would not implicate him.

Pierre calmed down and took another sip of the red wine. On second thoughts, Penfolds Grange Shiraz 2015 was a good vintage, even better than 2012. But he wouldn't tell Michelle about his new conclusion. Pierre had already given an order, and for this command, Pierre was ready to live with the consequences.

Pierre smiled as he anticipated his 'suffering' on the way home. Life could be worse!

Chapter 23: The UN summit outbreak. 13th of May 2021.

Pierre Beaumont chewed a few Brazil nuts and got on the stage in front of the assembled delegates. It was time to shine. Pierre was giving a presentation on how the World Bank was going to 'help' developing countries affected by the Coronavirus lockdowns that occurred the previous year. In reality, the World Bank had never, ever, helped any country, and the places that received their subsidies stayed poor indefinitely. Pierre's speech slurred, as he feared that he had revealed the World Bank's true intentions. Judging from the lack of reactions from the crowd he hadn't. Or maybe they already knew, but they didn't care, as long as they could enrichen themselves. Pierre studied the gathered world leaders. All the prominent ones were present.

- Chairman Jing Xi from China
- President Deidrick Dump from the USA
- Chancellor Angela Mittler from Germany
- Prime Minister Scurry Morrissett from Australia.

Would any of them survive the outbreak? It was crucial that Jing Xi survived. It would be hard to pin the blame on him for the outbreak if he died.

Pierre feared that the outbreak could cause a nuclear war. Neither he, nor the World Bank would win if things escalated to a nuclear exchange. An economic collapse was what Pierre needed, but people were unpredictable and things could go out of hand. For a second, Pierre thought about contacting Vladimir and tell him to not contaminate the drinking water. But if he didn't move ahead with the attack, he would lose all his money and owe billions. In such a scenario, jail time was the best possible outcome for Pierre.

Pierre made up his mind. He would proceed as planned. The fear that he experienced was only his conscience messing with his mind. After a bit of mumbling, he continued his presentation.

JING XI WAS LISTENING to Pierre Beaumont's presentation. He wondered what the bloody idiot was talking about. Pierre didn't follow the presentation notes, and he was rambling incoherent nonsense. Jing shrugged his shoulders. He didn't care about the presentation. But the number of diseased people among the crowd would be a good distraction from the main event that was to take place in Xuwan. Jing ate his fifth nut and coughed loudly. Since the Hei Bai virus was airborne and extremely contagious, this would be enough to infect everyone in the room. Once the outbreak began, it would implicate the USA as Deidrick Dump wouldn't get infected while other world leaders, who were against Dump, would.

Pierre paused his presentation and spoke to Jing:

- Chairman Xi. Are you okay?

Jing:

- No, I am not. I need to return to my hotel at once!

Everyone in the room stared at Jing as he got up and walked out of the room. Jing braced himself. The rash was getting painful, but it wasn't dangerous to him as he had antibodies from several other Hei Bai virus episodes.

"Get me to my hotel suite, and make sure that the cameras are ready for my statement," Jing commanded his bodyguards and he left the UN headquarters together with them.

PIERRE FINISHED HIS presentation and he hurried to leave the venue. What a disaster the presentation had been. Pierre brushed off some imaginary dust from his jacket. Although he felt like a fool, he would feel marvellous once his plan had come into fruition. Pierre texted Vladimir. "Did you complete the mission?" A few minutes later he received a "Yes."

Pierre got up. He needed to attend a meeting at the Federal Reserve, where the real power resided. Besides, Pierre didn't want to be at the UN headquarters when people started collapsing around him. When the outbreak took place, Pierre would much rather follow the figures on his trading screen. He got excited thinking about how his shorting of the market would propel him towards unparalleled wealth. Pierre got into the limousine that took him to the Federal Reserve.

PIERRE WAS ATTENDING a seminar at the Federal Reserve Bank of New York. Angus Brothschild was explaining how the federal reserve could print more money and give to the wealthy to stimulate the economy. Pierre agreed with the notion but he found listening to Angus dull and boring. Angus was an intellectual lightweight. The only reason that he was the head of the Federal Reserves' New York branch was that he was heir to the Brothschild throne. Pierre wasn't a fan of the hereditary transition of power. It allowed imbeciles to rise to the top instead of promoting talent. Pierre wasn't born wealthy. He had clawed his way to the top, reaching the top spot through murdering his rival Chakri Apinya. That was the true spirit of nature, to do anything to reach one's goal!

Pierre got interrupted from his daydreaming when the man next to him, the vice-chancellor of the European central bank, turned sick. Was the man infected by the Hei Bai virus? How could that be? While Pierre could have infected him, he hadn't seen the man eat any selenium-rich food to activate the disease.

Angus:

- Are you okay, Jurgen?

Jurgen:

- My back. It is on fire.

"Oh shit. Here we go." Pierre thought. But how had this happened? Had Jurgen eaten some high-selenium food before attending the meeting? That would be some bad luck! Suddenly, the man opposite Pierre collapsed to the floor as well. "I feel so hot, please help me."

Pierre realised that he needed to get out of the room. His intention had failed and somehow, he was killing his fellow bankers. Even though he didn't care about their lives, he didn't want to end up in quarantine. It was crucial that he didn't. He couldn't implement his trading schemes if he was in hospital lockup and all his plans could come to naught.

Pierre rushed out of the room and into the bathroom. He inserted his Zetan monocle, set it to avoid confrontation, and left the Federal Reserve building.

"Vladimir, meet me at the airport at once. We are heading back to Geneva straight away." Pierre texted. Pierre got back to his limousine. His driver was lying on the ground next to the car, screaming in pain. "Fuck this shit." Pierre thought and shouted:

- Give me your keys now. I need to get back to the airport straight
away.

Driver:

- Please help me. The pain is unbearable!

Pierre:

- Give me the keys, and I'll drive you to the hospital.

Driver:

- Here. Take them.

The driver handed Pierre the keys. Pierre scoffed at him.

- Bloody useless. Did you really think that I would drive YOU?

The driver wheezed something in return but Pierre didn't bother to respond. Instead, he drove as fast as he could to the airport. It wasn't easy. The city had descended into complete chaos. Dead and dying were lying everywhere. How had this happened?

JING XI HAD FINISHED recording the video showing how the Americans had poisoned him when he suspected that something was amiss. The endless sirens of emergency vehicles and screaming were making the city surreal. Jing looked outside the window. There were several Hei Bai virus infected people outside on the street and it seemed that the army was gathering in hazmat suits.

Jing turned on the TV. The news reporter said. "There is a biological warfare attack in New York. Most world leaders attending United Nations summit confirmed dead, including the US president Deidrick Dump."

Jing turned off the TV. This was a disaster. Jing had hoped to infect a few leaders that were enemies of the United States. This would have implicated the USA was behind the biochemical warfare attack that would take place in Xuwan. Jing called Tzi Cheng:

- Tzi Cheng. Something is amiss. New York has been hit hard by a Hei Bai virus attack. There is a change of plan. You have to abort the attack on Xuwan. We can no longer blame the US for an attack on China since the US president died himself from the virus. This is an atrocity!

Tzi Cheng stayed silent for a while and replied:

- It is too late. We have already contaminated the water supply in Xuwan a few hours ago.

Jing:

- Turn off the water in that city. Let's minimise the outbreak.

Tzi Cheng:

- If we close down our water supplies in Xuwan to stop the virus, the Americans will know that we released the virus in New York.

Jing sighed. Someone had played him and he was in trouble. But the situation was still salvageable. After all, Jing had been infected himself from the outbreak and the virus struck one of China's cities as well. Jing hoped that he could implicate a third party. Jing:

- Okay. You're right. Do nothing with the water supply. Release Jared next to Eileen's rally. He will seek her out. Then arrest them and everyone else that opposes us once the outbreak starts.

Tzi Cheng:

- Understood, Heavenly Master. I recommend that you leave the United States as fast as possible. Things are going to get nasty in New York.

Jing:

- Yes. I will get out of here straight away.

Jing hung up the phone, and he turned to his bodyguards:

- What are you waiting for, you idiots? We are leaving New York at once. Take me to the airport. And whatever you do, don't drink anything from the tap!

Having said this, the group got up and they all rushed towards the airport.

PIERRE BEAUMONT GOT on the plane, and he noticed that the pilot hadn't arrived. This was bloody inconvenient. He had saved his servant by warning about the tap water, but he hadn't saved his pilot. "That was a stupid way to prioritise!" Pierre muttered to himself.

Vladimir arrived at the aircraft and he looked happy, happier than Pierre had ever seen his Russian assassin and booty call. Pierre looked at Vladimir and spoke:

- What happened? Why was there an outbreak in the entire city? I only intended to infect the United Nations summit.

Vladimir smiled maliciously and replied:

- I went above and beyond your orders, Pierre.

Pierre stared at Vladimir with a mixture of terror and admiration. Pierre:

- WHAT exactly did you do, Vladimir?

Vladimir smirked:

- Well, after you told me about the mission, I had a thought. I thought: Why kill 500 when I can kill 500,000?

- So, I ordered 5 tonnes of selenium hydride, and I dumped it straight into New York's water supply.

- Then I walked around in the city and coughed at everyone while being infectious. You know how contagious this virus is. Muahaha!

Pierre:

- Bah, I don't advocate for needless killing. Killing 500 world leaders would have made me the same amount of money.

The intuitive interface of Pierre's monocle revealed that Michelle had overheard the conversation. "Fucking hell, such a hassle it will be to train a new waitress!" Pierre thought and shouted:

- Vladimir, Michelle overheard us. Seize her.

Michelle tried to escape from the dangerous Russian, but it was to no avail, and Vladimir subdued her.

Pierre:

- Drag her onto the plane. We'll deal with her there.

Vladimir dragged Michelle onto the plane. As they reached the inside of the plane, Michelle whimpered:

- Please spare me. I won't say anything. Think about my family.

Pierre shrugged his shoulders and replied:

- I am sorry, Michelle. You have been a good servant and I would love to spare you. But I am not willing to take the risk. Instead, you'll die from the Hei Bai virus like most of Manhattan. It will be painful and unpleasant, but I need an alibi.

Pierre took out some selenium hydride and dissolved it into a bottle of water. He handed the bottle to Vladimir and spoke.

- Michelle must be thirsty. Let's give her some water.

After that, Pierre and Vladimir force-fed Michelle from the bottle. Due to the extremely high selenium content in the water bottle, Michelle's symptoms spread fast. When Pierre was satisfied that Michelle would die, they threw Michelle out of the plane, closed the door and prepared for take-off. Pierre used the Zetan monocle to start the plane and took off. He didn't even bother to contact air traffic control to get permission to leave. The city had descended into chaos anyway.

JING XI ARRIVED AT the same private airport in New York. He saw how Pierre and Vladimir threw out the body of Michelle from their plane and then took off. Jing didn't reflect much over it. He needed to get out of the city himself.

Jing:

- Get my plane ready.

Jing's bodyguard, Ma Tin, shook his head and replied.

- I have tried calling our pilots. None of them is picking up. The outbreak must have infected them.

Jing panicked. He couldn't be stuck in this city. It was way too dangerous. Because after the deaths from the virus had subsided, the city would collapse into anarchy with the death of the US leadership. Jing:

- Come with me. We need to use the airport's public announcement system to look for a pilot.

Jing and his bodyguards entered the airport terminal. Dead and dying were littering the corridors. Jing approached the air traffic control room. The door was locked. Ma Tin took out his pistol and shot the lock to pieces. After that, he kicked in the door. Jing walked up to a microphone and made an announcement.

- Hello. This is Jing Xi, the president of China. I am willing to pay $1 million to any pilot that can pilot our plane away from this city. Please come to gate 12 to declare your interest.

Jing felt a deep sense of relief when a pilot showed up a few minutes later. He felt so relieved, so he didn't even object when the pilot insisted on flying to London instead of Beijing. After agreeing on the pilot's terms, Jing hurried to the plane that would take him away from the disaster-struck New York City.

Chapter 24: Go see your girlfriend, white devil! 14th of May 2021.

"Go see your girlfriend, Gweilo!" the Chinese soldier shouted at the Australian agent as he pushed Jared Pond out of the white van.

Hitting the asphalt with speed, Jared scraped his arms and knees, destroying his clothes and causing him to bleed profusely. Jared felt confused. He had never anticipated the CPOC operatives would let him out of this alive.

As Jared's arms and legs were bound with cable ties, Jared wriggled until he could find a sharp surface. Jared rubbed the cable ties against the curb until they broke and he was a free man.

Jared got up. He thought about what the guard had shouted to him. Why did the Columnist Party want him to find Eileen Lu? Jared realised that he had to play along with the dictatorship's plan. He was wounded and carried neither money nor a passport. This was hardly ideal circumstances, especially since he didn't even know where he was!

Jared walked up to a group of people playing mahjong and spoke:

- Where am I?

The people shook their heads, picked up their game, and left without acknowledging Jared. Jared couldn't blame them. They must have seen how the secret police had thrown him out of a moving vehicle and had assumed that any contact with him was dangerous. Jared was close to collapsing in self-pity when he heard a familiar voice:

- Jared, what happened to you?

Jared looked up and saw the angelic features of Eileen Lu. He felt dizzy and blissful at the same time. He had assumed that he would never get out of captivity alive, and yet here he was, together with Eileen. Jared:

- My boss betrayed me and sold me out to the Columnist Party. I don't know why they let me go.

Eileen:

- Oh my god, Jared. What did those monsters do to you? We need to get you out of China.

Jared:

- But I have no money and no passport.

Eileen:

- Come with me. I'll help you get to the Australian Consulate in Shanghai after the rally.

Eileen turned to one of her associates and spoke:

- Chen Lan, please help Jared. He'll need to walk with us, and then I'll take him with me to Shanghai.

Chen nodded and she helped Jared get back to his feet. As Jared got up, Eileen kissed him and spoke:

- I need to hurry to the rally. I am giving a speech. Chen will help you, and I'll meet you afterwards.

Jared:

- Thank you, Eileen.

Eileen rushed off to make her way to the civil liberties rally, while Chen helped Jared to a nearby apartment.

JARED WAS SITTING IN an apartment overlooking the main square of the city of Xuwan. Jared was listening to Eileen's speech, while Chen Lan was patching up his wounds. Chen:

- Do you want some tea?

Jared:

- No, thank you.

Chen:

- Okay. This is my third cup. I love tea.

Saying this, Chen went to the kettle and filled her cup with some more tea. Jared sighed. He couldn't understand why CPOC had released him and he worried that something was amiss. Why did Jing's goons want him to meet with Eileen?

- AH! My back is burning!

Jared turned towards Chen who was lying on the floor, screaming in pain. Jared:

- Get on your stomach and stay still.

Jared got up, grabbed a pair of scissors and cut up Chen's blouse. Chen's back was full of bark-like rash that was spreading quickly. Jared had an epiphany; this must be the same virus that he had seen in the video from the Uighur concentration camp. 'So, this is why they released me. To frame me for the outbreak!' Jared realised.

Jared realised that he needed to warn Eileen and the others for the outbreak before it was too late.

Chen wheezed:

- Help me. Don't leave me.

Jared looked at her for a brief moment, turned around, and left the apartment. He felt terrible for abandoning the woman who had patched up his wounds. Yet, if the Columnist Party aimed to murder the civil rights movement with the virus, there was no time to waste.

Jared got out from the apartment complex, and he ran towards the stage. When he was halfway to the stage, a man next to him collapsed to the ground. He was too late, but he had to save Eileen.

He got on the stage and shouted at Eileen:

- Chen is dead. Everyone needs to leave. The Columnist party has
  unleashed the Hei Bai virus on the crowd.

Eileen:

- What are you talking about?

Jared didn't have the time to answer, as one of the other civil rights leaders on the stage collapsed.

Eileen:

- Zhang Wei! What's happening to you?

Jared:

- Eileen! Tell everyone that they need to leave now. The Columnist
  Party is attacking us with biological warfare.

Eileen shouted out the message to the crowd, but they didn't get far. Hundreds of white vans and soldiers in hazmat suits arrived and sealed off all the exits to the square.

Some of the soldiers ran up to the stage and subdued Jared and Eileen, and threw them into an unmarked white van.

Chapter 25: Jing Xi kills his wife with the Hei Bai virus. 15th May 2021.

Jing Xi was back at his presidential palace in Beijing. The world was in an uproar after the Hei Bai virus outbreak in New York and Xuwan, and the global death toll was approaching half a million. Jing Xi had declared a national lockdown and it was time to wipe out the 1.2 million dissenters that Jing's AI had identified. They would all 'die from the virus' and the Columnist Party would add them to China's death toll during this 'tragic' time of Chinese history.

Even though everything was going according to plan, Jing felt worried. He could not be certain that the virus testing video was deleted from the internet. Jing needed a way to gain sympathy, a way to prove that he was not the mastermind behind the virus outbreak. Jing pulled his hair. He worried about the massive outbreak that had taken place in New York. Jing hadn't ordered the contamination of New York's water supply, so who was behind it?

Jing tapped up a bath and added some bath salts. A nice, warm, oily bath would soften his limbs and put his mind at ease. He thought of summoning Min Li. Jing intended to meet her for her company as he was too tense to think about sex. Jing sunk his fat body into the warm water and for a short moment, he felt at peace. The shrieking voice of his wife, Lan Peng, broke the peace.

- Honey. Are we still going to the Shen Yun dance show?

Jing took a deep breath. Why would he even consider visiting the Shen Yun dance show? Jing's enemies, The Falun Gong movement, sponsored the Shen Yun performers. Jing:

- Are you fucking insane? Why would I visit the dance show run by my enemies during a nationwide lockdown?

Lan Peng:

- Do we need a lockdown every time you hype a flu virus? Lah? Last year was so boring!

Jing:

- 200,000 people died in Xuwan yesterday. It is not hyped this time. You stupid bitch!

Lan Peng:

- Whatever, lah. I'll ask Chancellor Chi Wang to summon the Shen Yun troupe for a private show. He knows how to treat me.

Hearing this, reminded Jing of his suspicions that Lan Peng was cheating on him with Chi Wang. He had suspected it for years, but he had never bothered investigating. After all, he was too busy having sex with his young and beautiful concubines to pay his wife's sex life any attention.

But, since Lan Peng was cheating on him, he had a reason to murder her. If she were to die from the Hei Bai virus, Jing could showcase his tragedy to the world. That would deflect suspicions elsewhere. Jing smiled. It was time to fulfil the 'until death do us apart' part of his wedding vows and send Lan Peng off to the afterlife!

JING XI APPROACHED Lan Peng as she was preparing her make up for her private Shen Yun dance show. He gave her a cup of tea laced with selenium and spoke:

- I am sorry, honey-boo. You were right. I would be happy to watch the Shen Yun show together with you.

Lan Peng:

- Oh really? What made you change your mind?

Jing:

- I am not a fan of leaving you alone with Chi Wang. He might make a fool out of himself swooning over your beauty.

Lan Peng scoffed:

- Bah. When was the last time you called me beautiful?

Jing:

- I just did. Now stop arguing.

Lan Peng:

- What about Min Li and your other whores?

Jing:

- You cannot expect the Emperor of China to settle for one old hag. Now drink your tea and we'll head to the show. I am not going to ask again.

Lan Peng thought of objecting but she didn't. Instead, she had a few sips of the tea and replied:

- Thank you, for giving me the tea, Heavenly Master.

Jing smiled as Lan drank the tea, he watched her for a while. Eventually, he spoke:

- I know what you did. I know that you have been fucking Chi Wang behind my back for years.

Lan Peng:

- So, what is it to you? Since when do you care about my fidelity?

Jing:

- It's not about fidelity. It's about power. I cannot have my chancellor fuck my wife.

- On the bright side, you will realise that the Hei Bai virus is very real, as it ends your life in terrible pains.

Lan was about to slap Jing when the virus took hold of her and she collapsed to the ground in severe pain. Lan shouted:

- What did you do to me, monster?

Jing:

- I infected you with the Hei Bai virus.

- I'll use your death to my advantage. I'll get my revenge for your affair with Chi Wang, and I can use your passing as a distraction. I will fill all the newspapers with stories about how I am mourning your tragic death.

Lan Peng couldn't argue against Jing Xi. Her excruciating pain took hold of her senses and all she could do was to scream in pain. After a few minutes, the pain put Lan into shock. She slipped into unconsciousness never to wake up again.

Chapter 26: Pierre Beaumont witnesses Lan Peng's murder via the hacked AI. 15th May 2021.

Pierre Beaumont was lying in bed with his assassin and occasional lover, Vladimir Kravchenko. Pierre studied the naked body of his dangerous and muscular lover. A chilling thought struck Pierre: Vladimir had killed 100's of thousands in New York and nothing stopped him from murdering Pierre as well. Pierre thought of striking first. There would never be a better opportunity to kill the cold-blooded Russian than now, and Pierre had a good motive. Vladimir's action had caused two of Pierre's fellow bankers at the Federal Reserve meeting to die.

Pierre looked at the pistol that lay on the bedside table next to Vladimir. With a bit of luck, he could reach the pistol and shoot Vladimir in his sleep. There was, however, a problem. Vladimir had his Zetan monocle connected and its intuitive processing would alert Vladimir if Pierre became a threat. If it came to violence, Pierre would be dead. Vladimir had carried out hundreds of assassinations in the last year, while Pierre had been counting money in his ivory tower.

Pierre shook off his murderous plans and checked his trading accounts. The attack on New York had turned Pierre into a trillionaire. It wasn't his personal wealth. It was the wealth of the letterbox companies that he controlled, which was just as well. Pierre pondered whether he was the wealthiest man on the planet. It was hard to tell, as many wealthy individuals hid their wealth using trusts, offshore companies, and other instruments.

Pierre's Zetan Monocle beeped and Pierre connected it to his eye. Pierre rejoiced over what he saw. A video showed how Jing Xi murdered his wife in cold blood. This was excellent news. With even more evidence against China and Jing Xi, Pierre could soon crush Jing Xi, and get away with his crimes. The demise of China would make him the richest and mightiest person in the world and everyone would bow to him.

Pierre slapped Vladimir and exclaimed:

- Vladimir! Wake up, you big bear! Check out the latest video from China. My great plan is coming into fruition.

Vladimir watched the video and shook his head:

- Why do I care if Jing Xi killed his wife?

Pierre:

- Because these are damning evidence against Jing. Combine this with the virus testing video and Jing and the Columnist Party leadership will fall.

Vladimir:

- If they fall, they will bring the world down with them. Do you want a nuclear war?

Pierre took a deep breath and walked a few steps away from the bed. Vladimir was correct. If he exposed the crimes of the Chinese leadership the nuclear option would be on the table, and all his hard-won victories would be for nothing. He would need to eliminate the Chinese leadership, and Pierre had an idea.

Pierre turned to Vladimir and spoke:

- Vladimir. Head to the airport at once. I have a mission for you in China. There is someone that I need you to meet.

Vladimir:

- Understood. I'll leave at once.

After saying this, Vladimir got dressed and headed towards the airport. Meanwhile, Pierre remained in his mansion and prepared the next step of his plan.

Chapter 27: Jing Xi is taunting Eileen when he gets an urgent reminder. 16th May 2021.

Eileen Lu was confined in a damp and dark prison cell, in a Ministry of State Security facility in Beijing. She realised that she wouldn't get out of this alive. However, what worried her the most was the carnage she had witnessed before the secret police had arrested her. Several people in her movement had collapsed to the ground showing symptoms of the Hei Bai virus. Had Jing Xi unleashed a deadly virus on the Chinese population? That was a new low, even for him.

Eileen heard some ruckus from the outside corridor and the door opened. It was a group of guards that pushed a bruised and battered Jared into the cell. Tzi Cheng:

- We fetched your boyfriend for you, Eileen.

Eileen:

- What did you do to him?

Tzi Cheng:

- We gave him a taste of Columnist Party hospitality.

- Freshen up, Eileen. Chairman Xi is coming and he doesn't like dirty people.

After saying this, Tzi Cheng and the guards left and slammed the door behind them.

Eileen rushed over to Jared who was delirious and passing in and out of consciousness. Eileen:

- Jared. What did they do to you?

Jared slurred:

- Eileen? I don't know, but I feel dizzy. At least we'll die together. I love you.

After saying this, Jared passed out and Eileen had to face her fears alone.

JING XI AND TZI CHENG entered the cell an hour later. Jing looked around in the cell and scoffed at Tzi Cheng:

- I cannot fuck her in here. Bring them to a nice cell.

Tzi Cheng shouted:

- Guards. Bring them to the rape room.

A few sturdy guards came in and they dragged Eileen and Jared to a much nicer cell. Once they were in the luxurious prison cell, Jing spoke again.

- Awaken the Australian spy. I want him to be fully aware.

Tzi Cheng injected Jared with a shot of adrenaline and Jared woke up with a shock, gasping for air. Jared stared at Jing and spoke:

- Dictator Jing Xi? Why on Earth are you here?

Jing nodded at Tzi Cheng, and Tzi Cheng punched Jared's in the kidneys. Tzi Cheng:

- It's chairman Jing Xi. Say it right, Australian dog.

Jared realised that debating Jing's title wasn't worth another punch to the kidneys so he replied:

- Chairman Jing Xi. What brings me the honour.

Jing smirked:

- I have no interest in you, dog. The beautiful and fiery Eileen Lu is the reason that I am here. I will tame her like I tame everyone else.

Eileen:

- Don't touch me, you fucking creep.

Jing punched Eileen in the face and then he laughed:

- How funny is that? This girl is giving the chairman of China orders? I don't think so.

Eileen didn't reply and Jing spoke again:

- I was going to present you with good news. As your host, I will provide you with fresh food and drinks.

- Yet, there is a slight problem. We have contaminated the food and drinks with selenium. So, if you eat or drink, you'll activate the Hei Bai virus that lies dormant in your bodies. If you don't, you'll thirst to death.

Eileen shouted at Jing:

- Do you want me to beg for mercy? It's never going to happen. Just kill us already, you evil monster!

Jing:

- I am not going to kill you yet. I have been longing for months to force my manhood upon you. The time has finally come. Make yourself ready, Eileen.

Tzi Cheng and the other guards chained Eileen against the bed with her facing down. Jing snorted some Viagra and was about to rape Eileen when an urgent message popped up on his phone. The AI had identified Chancellor Chi Wang to be an enemy of Jing and the Columnist Party. Jing showed Tzi Cheng the notification and Tzi Cheng nodded. Jing turned to Eileen and spoke:

- We'll have to make love later. I have an urgent party business to attend to.

Having said this, Jing and Tzi Cheng left the room in a hurry.

Chapter 28: Enemy of the State. 16th May 2021.

Jing Xi, Tzi Cheng, and a group of bodyguards were heading for Chancellor Chi Wang's office in the Chinese Presidential Palace. It was imperative to deal with Chi Wang at once. If the second most powerful person in the country had turned hostile, the whole nation was at risk.

As Jing entered the office, Chancellor Chi Wang and a group of bodyguards stood ready. They aimed their pistols at Jing's group who followed suit, and it all ended in a deadlock. Chi Wang screamed at Jing Xi.

- I saw the video. You murdered Lan Peng through infecting her with the Hei Bai Virus.

Jing:

- Don't lie. The death of my wife was a great tragedy that has shaken me to the core. Don't deflect the fact that the AI identified you as an enemy of the state.

Chi Wang:

- It has also identified you as an enemy of the people, so that means nothing. Don't let a stupid AI determine who is right and who is wrong.

Jing:

- Really? Show me where it says that I am an enemy of the people.

Chi Wang:

- It's all in the system.

After saying this, Chi Wang handed Jing a tablet, which was logged in to the core system of the AI supervising China.

Jing pretended to look at the tablet for a few seconds, and then he shouted "Now!". Hearing this, Tzi Cheng swiftly shot Chi Wang and Chi Wang's bodyguards. Jing picked up the tablet again, and he overrode the code that classified him as an enemy of the people. Jing turned to Tzi Cheng and spoke:

- Check if he is still alive.

Tzi Cheng kneeled beside Chi Wang, checked his pulse and nodded:

- Yes, Chairman Xi. The traitor Chi Wang is still alive.

Jing dissolved some selenium hydride in a water bottle and replied:

- Give him something to drink. It is better if Chi Wang dies as an unfortunate victim of the Hei Bai virus.

Tzi Cheng did as Jing instructed and infected every enemy that was still alive with the Hei Bai virus. As Jing watched Chi Wang die from the Hei Bai virus he called Dr Song Bao:

- Chancellor Chi Wang has fallen victim to the Hei Bai virus. I command you to come and verify the cause of his death. Don't bring anyone else.

Dr Song Bao:

- Did he really die from the Hei Bai virus?

Jing:

- He died with the Hei Bai virus in his body. Wasn't that how we agreed to count Coronavirus deaths that we dispersed last year?

Dr Song Bao:

- Understood, Chairman Xi.

Jing hung up the phone and turned to Tzi Cheng:

- Investigate why Chi Wang accused me of murdering my wife. I fear that someone is trying to sow dissent in the Columnist Party.

Tzi Cheng:

- Did you murder your wife, Jing?

Jing gave Tzi Cheng a cold dead stare and replied:

- Yes. She was fucking Chi Wang behind my back. But I want to know how he found out about it.

Tzi Cheng:

- Understood. We will investigate his phone and computer.

Jing:

- Good. Make sure to be discrete. This situation could lead to the fall of the Columnist Party. If the party falls, so will you, Tzi Cheng!

Tzi Cheng nodded and replied.

- You'll have our discretion.

Jing:

- Good. I am heading home. I am an old man and I need to drink some tea with honey to relax from all this stress.

After saying this, Jing left the murder scene and headed home. On the way home, worries filled Jing's mind. How did Chi Wang know about how Jing murdered his wife, and why had the AI tagged Jing as an enemy of the people?

Chapter 29: We need to save Eileen Lu from Columnist Party detention. 16th May 2021.

Pierre Beaumont was drinking a glass of Chateau Margaux 2000 red wine and listening to Chopin - Nocturne op.9 No.2 in front of the fireplace in his mansion. It was a warm evening and it was ridiculous to run the air-conditioning and the fireplace at the same time, but Pierre enjoyed the setting. Pierre had his Zetan monocle lying on the coffee table. While he enjoyed the heightened intelligence it provided, he needed to unwind every now and then and have the mind of a human, a lesser species.

The monocle beeped to warn for danger, and Pierre was about to insert it, but he was too late. "Freeze! Hold it right there!" An American voice commanded.

Pierre got startled, spilled wine over his shirt, and turned around. CIA agent James Winter was aiming a silenced pistol at him. Pierre:

- Did you injure my guards?

James:

- There was no need. I hacked the house's security system and my monocle made it easy for me to infiltrate the house undetected.

Pierre:

- That's a relief. It's such a pain to find good employees these days.
- Why are you here, James?

James:

- I want you to tell me about your involvement in the biological weapon attack on New York.

Pierre:

- I don't know what you are talking about.

James:

- Yes, you do. I know that you and the World Bank made an absolute fortune from shorting the international markets before the attack.

Pierre sighed. He realised that he hadn't hidden his tracks well enough if James Winter had found out. However, James had heightened intelligence via his Zetan Monocle, so Pierre hoped that the other dimwits wouldn't realise. Pierre:

- You are right, James.

- I knew about the attack in advance and I chose to benefit from it. But I was never involved in the attack.

James:

- So, who is behind the attack?

Pierre:

- Jing Xi and agents from the Columnist Party.

James:

- Do you have any evidence?

Pierre:

- Yes. I have these videos. I also have reports showing that Jing Xi bought five tonnes of Selenium Hydride to contaminate the New York water supply.

James:

- How do you know all this?

Pierre:

- I own the company that is maintaining the Chinese government's surveillance AI. I have backdoors into their systems and I know everything they are up to.

James:

- Wow. This is amazing.

Pierre:

- Yes. Now put that gun away. You are making me uncomfortable.

James put away the pistol and looked at the files and videos that Pierre had provided him with. James' Zetan monocle indicated that the documents and videos were genuine.

After a while, James sighed:

- Wow. This is explosive stuff. I would have hoped that some less powerful terrorist group had released the virus. A biological warfare attack from China. This will lead to war.

Pierre:

- I didn't know that the CIA was so afraid of war. You have started quite a few in the last few decades.

James scoffed:

- Bah. That's different. Bombing Iraq, who didn't have any weapons of mass destruction, is a lot less risky than attacking China. China is armed to the teeth and has a large nuclear arsenal!

Pierre:

- What if I can help you out?

James:

- What would you do?

Pierre:

- I can access the Chinese AI and designate Jing Xi and other top-ranking Columnist Party officials as enemies of the state. Then we can watch as they kill each other.

James:

- Hmm. Any chance that you can free Eileen Lu from her imprisonment?

Pierre:

- Eileen Lu? Who is that?

James:

- Eileen Lu is the most prominent leader in the Chinese civil rights movement. I suspect that the Columnist Party arrested her during the outbreak in Xuwan.

Pierre:

- And why do you want to free her?

James:

- Because if we can make her the president of China, China will become a weak pushover. Eileen is meek and a lot of the old guard would hate her. She would be completely dependent on foreign help to stay in power. Wouldn't that suit the Bank?

Pierre reached for his monocle and he inserted it. He pulled up Eileen's file and analysed it. Pierre realised that James was correct. Pierre had never considered installing a weak president in China to strengthen his power. His original plan had only entailed carrying out the bioweapon attack on New York to crash the markets and expand his wealth. But James had brought a new interesting scenario to the table.

Pierre accessed the Chinese AI and he found a video feed of Eileen in a prison cell together with the Australian spy, Jared Pond. Pierre didn't know why the Chinese had placed them in the same cell, but it wasn't particularly important. Pierre spoke:

- I am in on your plan. I'll instruct my agents to save Eileen. Furthermore, I will mark all the Columnist Party leadership as 'enemies of the state' in their AI. Then we can watch from afar how they are killing each other hoping to rise to power!

James:

- Excellent. I am sure that this will please President Mitchell Cent, who replaced Deidrick Dump when he died.

- Are you going to release the documents proving China's guilt?

Pierre:

- Yes. The compensation claims will drive them bankrupt and the Dragon will fall.

James:

- And the Banker will rise?

Pierre:

- Exactly!

James:

- Are you sure that you had nothing to do with the New York out-break?

Pierre:

- Don't ask questions you don't want answered. Now get out of my house. Leave via the front door this time!

Pierre pressed a button on his phone and two bodyguards arrived. Pierre:

- Gerard, Philip. Escort James from my property. He is overstaying his welcome.

For a second, Pierre noticed how James' threat level increased to 'moderate', but he quickly returned to 'low'. Without a word, James got up and followed the guards away from Pierre's residence.
Pierre called Vladimir:

- Vladimir, we have a new objective. You need to get Eileen Lu out of the Ministry of State Security facility in Beijing.

Vladimir:

- Do you want me dead, Pierre?

Pierre:

- Yes. But that's not going to happen, is it?

Vladimir:

- Correct. I'll speak to our contact on the inside. I'll get her out. But why do you want to save Eileen? I thought Jing Xi was the objective.

Pierre:

- Jing Xi is still the objective. But James Winter wants to save Eileen and make her the puppet president of China. We got to keep James and the CIA happy.

Vladimir:

- Understood. I will get her out.

Vladimir hung up the phone and Pierre got changed. He was annoyed that he spilled his exquisite wine after James Winter had threatened him at gunpoint, but he would have to forgive James. Pierre was certain that James had proof against him that he would release if Pierre sent Vladimir to kill him. In the end, it was all good. Pierre was certain that he could also benefit from installing Eileen Lu as a puppet president of China.

Pierre returned to his armchair and enjoyed another glass of wine. He turned on the stereo and resumed enjoying classical music.

Chapter 30: Dying with his pants down. 17th May 2021.

Jing Xi met up with Tzi Cheng at the Ministry of State Security facility in Beijing. To his surprise his secretary Biyu Sang was also there. Jing turned to her and spoke:

- Biyu. What are you doing here?

Biyu:

- The presidential palace is under lockdown because of the Hei Bai virus deaths yesterday. So, I came here to work for you.

Jing sighed. He should have anticipated that the palace would be in lockdown after the Chancellor of China had died 'from the Hei Bai virus'. But what could he do? It would look very suspicious if he insisted to open the palace at this stage. Jing:

- Very well. Let's find you a room so you can carry out your duties. Do not disturb us. We have a very important prisoner to interrogate.

Biyu:

- Who is the prisoner?

Tzi Cheng:

- That's none of your business, stupid secretary!

Jing:

- Tzi Cheng. You cannot tell Biyu off. She is my secretary. I am the one reprimanding her!

Tzi Cheng:

- Understood, Heavenly Master.

Jing turned to Biyu:

- We are interrogating the number 1 enemy of China, Eileen Lu. We suspect that she and her Australian boyfriend was behind the Hei Bai virus outbreak in Xuwan.

Biyu:

- But you are the leader of China, Chairman Xi. You can leave the interrogation of Eileen to someone else.

Jing lashed out and slapped Biyu. Jing:

- Do not question me, Biyu. Now go make us some tea or I'll lock you up in one of those cells myself.

Biyu rushed off towards the pantry without saying a word. Jing turned towards Tzi Cheng:

- Let's go. It is time for me to force Eileen Lu into submission.

EILEEN LU WAS SITTING in a luxurious holding cell together with Jared Pond. The room was comfortable, but since it was the rape room of the genocidal dictator Jing Xi, neither Eileen nor Jared could appreciate it.

Eileen's thirst was driving her mad and she made her way to the drinks station, which looked very enticing to her. Eileen was about to open a bottle of water when Jared pulled her away.

Jared:

- Don't drink anything, Eileen. Remember what Jing said. Jing has contaminated the water and we'll get the Hei Bai virus if we drink it.

Eileen:

- He is playing with your mind, Jared. Besides what do you want to do? Stay here and die from dehydration? Sit tight until Jing comes back and rapes me? If I die from the Hei Bai virus, he can't rape me at least.

Jared:

- For all we know, Jing might be dead. Did you see the hurry that he left in? I bet that trouble is brewing within the Columnist Party.

Eileen:

- So, what do you suggest that we do?

Jared:

- We stay put and hope that someone comes by. If we can overpower the guards, we have a shot at escaping.

Eileen:

- That sounds like suicide.

Jared:

- Yes, but less suicidal than infecting ourselves with the virus.

Eileen:

- Very well. I'll stay away from the water for now. But I won't let you force me to thirst to death!

Jared nodded. From what he had seen, dying from the Hei Bai Virus was fairly quick, while dying from thirst took longer and caused more suffering.

Jared didn't have the time to ponder on the matter further as a group of guards entered the cell, subdued him and Eileen, and chained them to their beds.

JING XI ENTERED THE cell with a malicious smile on his face. "Get out of here, you dogs!" Jing commanded and everyone except for Tzi Cheng left the room. Jing turned to Eileen and spoke:

- You must be thirsty, Eileen.

- How lucky that I brought you some bottles of fresh, uncontaminated water.

After saying this, Jing took out a plastic bottle of water from his coat jacket and handed it to Eileen.

Eileen threw the bottle away and spoke:

- Why would I trust that this water is not contaminated, you monster?

Jing picked up the bottle, opened it, and drank a few sips:

- Would I drink the water, if I had poisoned it?

Eileen:

- So, what do you want?

Jing:

- I want you and Jared to admit that you caused the Hei Bai Virus outbreak that killed more than 200,000 people in Xuwan.

- Furthermore, I want you, Eileen Lu. I want your luscious body and your warm wet pussy. If you submit to me, I might even let you live and take my late wife's place.

Eileen:

- I would never let you have me, you filthy murderer!

Jing sighed:

- I guess not even the emperor of China can have everything he wants.

Jing picked up the uncontaminated water bottle, poured the water over Eileen's crotch, and spoke again:

- Well, this is unfortunate, but I'll have to rape you and kill you.

Jared:

- Stay away from Eileen, you filthy pig!

Tzi Cheng ran up to the chained Jared, kicked him in the face, and broke his nose. Tzi Cheng:

- Shut up, white devil!

Jared didn't respond as Tzi Cheng's kick had knocked him out.

Jing put out a line of white powder, which was Viagra mixed with ground rhino horn. After snorting the powder, he beat his chest while chanting in Chinese to stimulate his erection.

Jing was about to enter Eileen when he heard the muffled sound of a silenced pistol and felt a sharp pain. He turned around and to his shock, he saw his timid secretary Biyu Sang. "Fuck you, Jing!" was the last thing Jing heard before everything turned black.

Chapter 31: The escape from China. 17th May 2021.

Vladimir Kravchenko was overlooking the prison where the Columnist Party kept Eileen imprisoned. He heard a multitude of sirens and distant gunfire, and the army seemed to be out in full force. This wasn't ideal. Vladimir called Pierre to discuss the situation:

Vladimir:

- The situation is not good, Pierre. Beijing has descended into civil war and chaos.

Pierre:

- And how is that not good? The chaos will make it a lot easier for you to extract Eileen Lu from the prison facility and escape the city. You wouldn't be able to do that if everyone was looking for you. Now they are busy killing each other.

Vladimir:

- What did you do?

Pierre:

- I told them the truth!

Vladimir:

- The truth?

Pierre:

- I listed everyone in the Columnist Party as an enemy of the Chinese people, and I released the video of how Jing Xi murdered Chi Wang.

- Now they are all trying to kill each other to rise to the top. It's beautiful, isn't it?

- But enough talk. Tell Biyu to hurry up

Vladimir:

- Understood.

Vladimir hung up the phone and messaged Biyu: "Move now. I am covering the back entrance. Hurry up."

BIYU UNCHAINED EILEEN and Jared in the cell. Jared was dizzy from Tzi Cheng's forceful kick and he was bleeding profusely. Biyu turned to Eileen:

- We need to leave. Hurry up.

Eileen hurried over to Jared to help him up on his feet. Jared's concussion made it difficult for him to get up. Biyu:

- Leave him behind. We need to go.

Eileen:

- I am not leaving him. It is not who I am.

Biyu shook her head, but there was nothing she could do. She couldn't threaten the woman she was there to save.

Eventually, Jared got up and they left the room. Outside there were a few dead guards, all shot in the head with millimetre precision. Biyu:

- Pick up their guns but don't use them unless you have to. It's better if we remain stealthy.

The alarm in the building went off, and Biyu shouted:

- Never mind that. Pick up the guns and don't hesitate to use them. Hurry up.

Having said this, Biyu contacted Vladimir via her radio:

- Vladimir! Create a diversion!

Vladimir:

- Copy that.

VLADIMIR TURNED ON 'combat mode: maximum casualties' on his Zetan Monocle. The following stats came up. 'Estimated casualties: 150. Chance of Survival: 98 %. The chance for Eileen's survival 52 %'.

'I can live with that!' Vladimir thought, and he fired off a grenade that hit the middle of the courtyard. The grenade didn't hit anyone, but that was never the intention. Instead, Vladimir intended to blow up the gas pipes that ran under the courtyard. The guards fired at him, and Vladimir took cover, reloaded the grenade launcher and fired another grenade. The second grenade blew up the gas pipes and caused a massive explosion that set the whole area ablaze.

Vladimir contacted Biyu:

- Hurry up, run through the courtyard.

Biyu:

- The whole courtyard is on fire.

Vladimir:

- You'll survive running through fire for a few seconds. You won't survive fighting the guards that are approaching you from the inside of the building.

Biyu:

- Understood.

POOF *CLICK*

Biyu threw away her pistol as she ran out of ammunition. She could hear the bullets fired by her opponents hitting the wall behind her.

- Give me your rifle, and hurry through that door. I'll cover you

Eileen gave Biyu her rifle and she ran towards the door and she opened it. She squirmed when she saw the inferno outside. Eileen:

- We can't go out there.

Biyu:

- We'll have to. We can't hold them off for much longer.

Eileen felt a sharp breeze as a 50 calibre round passed narrowly to her ear and hit a Columnist Soldier at the far end of the corridor.

Vladimir radioed Biyu:

- I'll kill her myself if she doesn't hurry up. Go!

Biyu got up and Vladimir shot her through the shoulder without severing any arteries. The bullet continued and hit a soldier in the head.

Biyu:

- What the fuck, Vladimir.

Vladimir:

- I saved your life. All the soldiers are dead. Now hurry up and cross the fire-stricken square and meet me in this building.

Biyu pulled herself together and got to Eileen. Biyu:

- We need to get to the other side of the square.

Eileen whimpered:

- Through that fire? Your friend almost shot me.

Biyu:

- He did shoot me, but he knows what he is doing. Hurry up or we'll die.

Eileen nodded and she helped the concussed Jared and the crippled Biyu through the fire to the building on the other side of the square.

As they got through the fire and halfway across the square, Biyu heard another shot and saw a Chinese army helicopter crashing into a building.

Vladimir radioed her:

- Hurry up. Our odds of survival are shrinking by the second.

The trio managed to cross the square, and Vladimir was waiting for them and urged them to hurry into a van.

THE GROUP WAS ON VLADIMIR'S private jet headed towards Mongolian airspace when two Chinese fighter jets intercepted them. The radio buzzed and one of the fighter pilots communicated:

- Return to Beijing immediately or we'll shoot down this plane.

Jared sighed:

- Shit. We were so close to escaping China. Only a few minutes until the Mongolian border. What do we do?

Vladimir:

- We shoot down the fighter jets.

Jared:

- How?

Vladimir pointed at his 50-calibre sniper rifle.
Jared:

- Are you insane? How would you shoot down two fighter jets with a rifle?

Vladimir:

- Yes. I am crazy. But I live for these moments. If I succeed, it will be amazing. If I fail, I'll go down in a fiery explosion of glory. Whichever happens, I am happy!

Jared:

- Alright. Let's do this. What do you need?

Vladimir:

- Strap yourselves in, and be ready to pull me up.

After saying this, Vladimir attached himself to an abseiling harness and picked up the sniper rifle. He opened the door to the plane and jumped out, hanging a few metres under the plane. 'Shots almost impossible.' Vladimir's monocle displayed. "I like those odds!" Vladimir said to himself and aimed at the first pilot. He pressed the trigger and he noticed how the bullet shattered the windscreen of the plane, but he couldn't determine if he had hit the pilot.

Vladimir didn't have the time to reflect over this, as the second plane fired off a missile towards his plane. Vladimir acted instinctively. He shot the tip of the missile and caused it to detonate under the fighter jet. This blew up the hostile plane.

"Pull me up!" Vladimir shouted to Jared and a few seconds later he was back in the plane. They closed the door and they were gasping for air on the floor for a while. Eventually, Vladimir spoke:

- That's how you do it, Jared. Ha-ha

After saying this, Vladimir was rolling on the floor, filled with raging outbursts of excitement.

Chapter 32: Meeting between Pierre Beaumont, James Winter, and Eileen Lu. 18th May 2021.

Jared Pond woke up the following day in a private Swiss medical facility overlooking Lake Geneva. His head was still sore from the concussion and he had burns on his body from running through the inferno when escaping the Chinese prison. Yesterday's events felt so surreal. In particular, the episode where Vladimir shot down two pursuing fighter jets with a sniper rifle.

Jared pinched himself in the arm and realised that he was alive. He heard that someone was in the shower and he admired Eileen's naked slender body covered in bath foam.

Eileen saw him and teased:

- Don't stand there peeking, Jared. Come join me.

Jared shook his head and smiled:

- I will join you in a couple of days. I have some pretty bad burns on my body.

Eileen:

- Oh really? Weren't you the horny one after we escaped those assassins in Shanghai?

Jared:

- That was different. That time I was unhurt but full of adrenaline. There is nothing more arousing. Now I am jetlagged, have a broken nose and several burns on my body. Believe it or not, I am not a machine!

Eileen:

- Then I better order one from China!

Jared:

- No, don't do that.

Eileen smiled:

- Don't worry, Jared. I am a big fan of the Aussie kind.

- You stay here and rest. I need to attend a meeting with Pierre Beaumont of the World Bank.

Jared:

- The World Bank? What does he want?

Eileen:

- I don't know. I think he was the one who sent Biyu and Vladimir to save us.

Jared:

- Okay. That makes sense.

Eileen:

- I still can't believe that we got out of Jing's captivity alive. This feels like a dream.

Jared:

- Then live the dream. Jing Xi is dead and the Columnist Party is collapsing. This could be a new start for China and the World.

Eileen walked up to Jared, kissed him, and replied:

- You're right, Jared. I'll better get dressed and prepare for the meeting. Take care.

Having said this, Eileen put on some of the hospital clothes and left the room.

A WHILE LATER, EILEEN'S limousine dropped her off at Pierre Beaumont's mansion. Pierre's new butler, Jean, approached Eileen and bowed to her. Jean:

- Welcome, Mademoiselle Eileen. My name is Jean Valmont. Monsieur Pierre asked me to get you dressed for the meeting. Please come with me.

Eileen:

- Thank you, Jean.

Jean showed Eileen to a room full of expensive women's clothes. Eileen looked around and spoke in amazement:

- Wow. Does Pierre always have so many options for female visitors?

Jean:

- Monsieur Beaumont thinks a woman must look her best in a social setting. May I suggest the brown stiletto shoes, the black pants and the yellow blouse. I would recommend that you accompany the clothes with this diamond necklace.

Eileen:

- That would be great. But I am not used to wearing high heels since I am pretty tall.

Jean:

- Yes, but of course. Silly me. How about these blue ballerina shoes?

Eileen:

- That will be great. Thank you.

Eileen got changed and she studied herself in the mirror. She loved the outfit and the diamond necklace, but at the same time she looked tired and worn out, having escaped from captivity.

Eileen:

- Do I need makeup as well?

Jean:

- No. Monsieur Beaumont is aware of your current circumstances. Besides, excessive use of makeup ruins the skin.

- Please come with me.

Eileen followed Jean and she reached the grand hall of Palace Beaumont.

EILEEN ENTERED THE grand hall of Palace Beaumont. It was newly built but the architecture borrowed many elements from the renaissance. Large panorama windows faced the lake below. Two men approached Eileen, and she noticed that they wore the same kind of monocle that Vladimir wore. Eileen studied the men. One of them was good-looking. He was a tall and muscular army guy with a crewcut hairstyle. The other man was balding and ugly with features that only a mother could love. The ugly man spoke to Eileen:

- Welcome to Palace Beaumont. I am Pierre Beaumont the CEO of the World Bank, and this is James Winter from the CIA.

Eileen:

- Nice to meet you, Pierre. I am Eileen Lu from the Chinese Civil Rights movement.

James:

- Yes, we know who you are.

Eileen:

- So, was it the CIA that freed me from China? I thought Vladimir was Russian?

James:

- The CIA has a widespread spy network and people of every nationality works for us. Vladimir Kravchenko, however, works for your host, Pierre Beaumont.

Pierre:

- Yes. Vladimir is the best in the world at what he does. Something I am sure that you have already noticed. I only hire the best. That is why I hope to associate with you.

Eileen nodded with an afterthought and replied:

- So, what exactly do you want me to do?

Pierre:

- Take it easy, Eileen. Please have a glass of red wine and come with me on a tour of my palace.

Eileen objected:

- It's 10 in the morning. Isn't it a bit early for wine?

Pierre:

- You would have died yesterday if I didn't intervene. Please accept my hospitality and the excellent vintage.

Eileen accepted the red wine and she acknowledged Pierre's request. Pierre guided her around the castle and he spoke about the different artworks that he had acquired on auctions recently. The guided tour stressed Eileen. She knew that Pierre had saved her for a reason and she wanted to find out why. Eventually, Eileen spoke:

- Pierre, I love your artworks and your passion for history. But you saved me for a reason and I need to know why.

Pierre cringed for a moment. He hated how Eileen had interrupted him when he spoke about the arts. He couldn't believe that James wanted to make such an arrogant bitch the new leader of China. Then again, James Winter was American, the birthplace of McDonald's, not the birthplace of classical music.
Pierre pointed to James and spoke:

- Bah. I saved you to help James and my American friends. James, please brief Eileen on what you expect from her.

James, who had remained silent during Pierre's guided tour, spoke:

- The Columnist Party is collapsing and their reign of terror is over. We will release evidence that Jing Xi was behind the outbreaks in New York and Xuwan.

- But we need to find a way forward to stabilise China. I believe you could be that way.

Eileen:

- What would you have me do?

James:

- There will be a global intervention to stop the budding civil war in China. After we have stopped the fighting, China will need an interim president. I want you to be that president.

Eileen:

- But you can't make me the president of China?

James:

- No, but President Mitchell Cent can. China killed a large number of world leaders at the United Nations summit in New York. The World and the Chinese Population will stand united against the remnants of the Columnist Party. You can lead the transition process. You will need to admit China's guilt, pay compensations, and dismantle the People Liberation Army.

Eileen:

- So, I will become the CIA's puppet president?

James:

- Yes, but you'll get what you want, and you'll avoid a global catastrophe.

Eileen sighed. She had wanted to free China from the Columnist Party, but she had never intended for western powers to humiliate her country. This would be a replay of the Opium Wars in the 19th Century. But Eileen understood why the world was vindictive after what had happened. Placating the world was the only way to save the Chinese people from complete destruction.

Eileen:

- I accept your proposal and I am willing to pledge my loyalty to President Mitchell Cent.

James:

- Excellent. I will make the arrangements.

- Please return to the medical facility and spend some time with your boyfriend. We have some busy days ahead of us.

After hearing this, Pierre rang a bell and a servant appeared. Pierre:

- Jean. Please take Mademoiselle Lu back to the Villeneuve Medical Facility.

Eileen nodded and she left Palace Beaumont.

Chapter 33: Bending One Knee to Theocracy. 22nd May 2021.

E ileen orgasmed and she got off her tireless lover, Jared Pond. Jared giggled at her:

- Are you tired already, Eileen? That was only 20 minutes.

Eileen:

- We need to prepare ourselves for meeting President Mitchell Cent.

Jared became more serious and replied:

- Yes, I know.
- How do you feel about all this?

Eileen:

- I feel terrible for all the deaths in my country. If I had bowed to Jing's tyranny many of those who've died would have been alive today. But on the other hand, what is the price of freedom?

Jared:

- It's a tough question.

- But don't feel guilty. It was Jing who chose to murder people with a new virus instead of debating politics. You can't allow yourself to cave in, to a tyrant like that.

Eileen:

- Yes. But even if I do become the president of China, I will still take orders from the USA and the World Bank. Am I then a president representing the people?

Jared:

- You can be the custodian paving the path for the one who will liberate China. Your goal was to liberate China. It can still happen in time. But you won't be the liberator.

Eileen:

- I guess you're right. For now, I must work to bring stability and save my fellow Chinese citizens.

Jared:

- And do you know what the best thing about it is?

Eileen:

- No?

Jared:

- That I will be there for you on every step of your journey.

Eileen:

- Thank you, Jared.
- Let's head to the White House. We are meeting with Mitchell Cent soon.

Jared:

- I can't wait to hang out with that religious nutcase! But let's go.

After this, Jared and Eileen had a quick shower, got dressed and took a limousine to the White House.

EILEEN LU FELT A BIT uncomfortable when she reached the White House. She noticed that Mitchell Cent had erected a large crucifix in the Oval Office. Furthermore, he had placed a baptism chalice with water on a pedestal next to the crucifix.

Mitchell approached Eileen and spoke:

- Welcome to America. The nation of God.

Eileen:

- Thank you for receiving me, President Cent.

Mitchell:

- Miss Lu. Do you profess in our Lord, Jesus Christ?

Eileen:

- I don't follow any religion, President Cent.

Mitchell:

- You must. As a man of God, I can only help you if you do!

Eileen glanced at Jared and he nodded. Eileen sighed:

- Very well. If I must embrace Christianity to save China, so be it. I profess to Jesus Christ.

Mitchell:

- Excellent. I will baptise you at once.

Mitchell Cent splashed some water on Eileen and started chanting verses from the Bible. After half an hour, he shook Eileen's hand, blessed her, and he left the office.

After Mitchell had left the room, James Winter approached Eileen and whispered:

- Don't worry, Eileen. Mitchell's presidency is just to appease the stupid masses. Other people run the country in the background.

James' words didn't encourage Eileen. It drained her motivation realising that the President of the USA was a showpiece, while other people ruled the country in the background. This crushed her illusions. Her successful fight against Jing Xi had been for nothing.

Eileen hid her disappointment and replied:

- Of course, James. I am happy to discuss what steps we can take to ensure China's future.

James:

- Excellent. Come with me. There are better places to discuss our plans. The White House has too many prying eyes.

Eileen and Jared got up to follow James Winter who turned around and spoke to Jared:

- Nothing personal, Jared, but my associates want to speak to Eileen alone. Not everyone is keen to speak to an Australian Spy.

Eileen turned to Jared:

- It's okay, Jared. I will see you at the hotel later.

After saying this, she kissed Jared and left the room together with James.

Chapter 34: Eileen Lu Becomes a Puppet President for China. 15th June 2021.

A steamy summer day, a few weeks later, Eileen and Jared were in Beijing. Eileen was about to become the president of China, representing her party, the Chinese Civil Rights Movement. They had landed a few days earlier, accompanied by a large NATO force supported by every country, including Russia and Iran. The attack on the UN summit had killed leaders from every country, even former allies of China. This, combined with the infighting among the Columnist Party leadership, meant that China was powerless to fight. Thus, there was no resistance to the invasion aimed at punishing the Chinese leadership for their crimes against humanity.

Jared entered Eileen's room and he noticed that she was crying:

- What's wrong, Honey.

Eileen:

- What is not wrong? I have landed in my home country escorted by a large foreign army. I have sold out China to foreign invaders. This was not how I envisioned the new China without the Columnist Party.

Jared:

- What if your dream was unrealistic? The Columnist Party would never give up without a fight. But with most of their leadership dead from infighting, they couldn't mount a defence against a foreign intervention.

Eileen:

- I know.

Jared:

- And at least you saved most of your followers from Jing Xi. If you hadn't acted, they would all be dead now. There was nothing more you could have done.

Eileen:

- I know. Life goes on. But I don't want to be the unelected president who carries out orders from foreign bankers.

Jared:

- I understand. But someone needs to govern China until there can be general elections. Would you rather have an American General running the country?

Eileen:

- I guess you are right.
- Hey. What do you think about these robes?

Eileen walked over to a mannequin that featured yellow and red silk robes with intricate patterns.
Jared:

- They are very fancy, but they don't look very stateman like.

Eileen:

- I think you're wrong.

- This mantle is a replica of a dress worn by Wu Zetian of the Tang Dynasty. She was the only reigning empress in Chinese history. She rose from nothing to ruling China during its peak in the 7th Century.

- I want to follow her example and restore China's glory.

Jared:

- But wasn't Wu Zetian a bloodthirsty tyrant?

Eileen:

- It's hard to tell. No ruler believed in human rights during the 7th century. As the only female ruler in Chinese history, she would have scared a lot of men. But the fact that she rose from nothing, and became the only female ruler in Chinese history, has always inspired me.

Jared:

- Very well, Empress Eileen. You better get changed then.

Eileen:

- Yes, and I want you to wear the red robe. The red robe is for the consort of the ruler.

Jared:

- Consort? Is that what I am?

Eileen teased:

- That is, if you want to marry me?

Jared:

\- You're driving a tough bargain.

\- Okay my empress, let's restore China to glory.

After saying this, they got changed into their Tang Dynasty clothing. Dressed in the exquisite garments they headed to the podium where Eileen would give her inauguration speech.

Chapter 35: Failing to Tame the Dragon. 15th September 2021.

Pierre Beaumont was watching the news reports in his Swiss mansion and he sighed. Eileen Lu had turned out to be impossible to control. This was a bit disappointing for Pierre but not the end of the world. His original plan had been to release the virus, make a fortune from shorting the markets and then blaming China for what had happened. This had been a success, and Pierre was now the richest man on the planet. The failure to control China via Eileen Lu was only a minor setback.

Pierre's servant Jean entered Pierre's lounge room:

- Monsieur Beaumont. James Winter from the CIA is here to meet you.

Pierre sighed. Bloody James coming unannounced again. At least this time he didn't sneak in with a gun! Pierre:

- Okay, please tell him to meet me here!

Jean left the room. Pierre put on his monocle. It was time to pay back James for threatening him four months earlier. Pierre grabbed a pistol and he hid behind the door when James entered the room. Pierre got out and aimed the pistol at James. Pierre:

- Looks like I am the one holding the gun this time.

James smirked back:

- Hmm. A Beretta 92D weighs 900 grams when it's empty. Your pistol weighs 900 grams. Why are you aiming an empty pistol at me?

Pierre put down the pistol on a table and sighed:

- Why are you here, James?

James:

- Eileen Lu is proving to be uncooperative. She urged the US to withdraw our forces within the end of the month.

Pierre:

- So, Eileen Lu is proving to be more capable than we gave her credit. That's nothing to worry about. You win some and you lose some.

James:

- Don't be so casual about this. We cannot let China disappear from our sphere of influence!

Pierre:

- I beg to differ. For the bank, there is no reason to soothe your ego by appointing puppet presidents. All that matters is the money and influence we can yield from a country.

James:

- Well, I want you to send Vladimir to kill her.

Pierre:

- But I won't. Why don't you go yourself?

Pierre smirked. He knew that while James could go to China and carry out the assassination, he didn't share Vladimir's insane disregard for his own life.

James:

- I can't. If a US agent gets caught on that mission, it would risk nuclear war.

Pierre:

- Yes, and we wouldn't want that.
- Goodbye, James. I hope that our paths won't cross for a while.

James shook his head and slammed the door as he left.
After James had left, Vladimir entered the room from the other side of the building:

- He didn't seem happy. What did he want?

Pierre:

- He wanted me to send you to kill Eileen Lu.

Vladimir:

- What? After all the trouble that I had when I dragged her out of China four months ago! What is wrong with him?

Pierre:

- It's the clueless American way. They do this all the time. First, they fund ISIS and then they spend four years bombing ISIS. Three months ago, they installed Eileen Lu as their puppet president, and now they want a new one. Pathetic!

Vladimir:

- So, what is your new evil scheme then?

Pierre:

- Summon Theodore Ahmadi. We will use media to terrify people about the Hei Bai virus. We will use this fear to sell the harmful cure at a grossly inflated price! Muahaha

Vladimir:

- Yes, Pierre. I will summon him at once.

Vladimir left and Pierre got seated in a leather armchair and he smiled to himself. Pierre always found new ingenious ways of hoarding money, and it filled the void within him!

Chapter 36: Forcing the Cure. 18th September 2021.

Pierre Beaumont was sitting in his office studying the molecule model he had built to cure the Hei Bai virus. With the help of the enhanced intelligence from his Zetan monocle, Pierre had made a great discovery. Pierre had found that a high dosage of a proprietary molecule of Ammonium Molybdate Tetrahydrate could draw the dormant Hei Bai virus out of healthy cells and kill it. The problem was that the cure was much more dangerous than the disease. The Hei Bai virus lay dormant in the body unless someone had a very high selenium intake. Ammonium molybdate tetrahydrate, on the other hand, could cause liver failure and infertility in high doses. To kill the Hei Bai virus, one had to take a large dose of the drug.

Pierre had a trump on hand. The corrupt GHA director Theodore Ahmadi was looking for a new hand to feed him, now that the bribes had dried up after Jing Xi's demise.

Theodore entered Pierre's office, and Pierre met him cordially:

- Welcome, Theodore. It's so good to see you. I hope my tokens of appreciation for your hard work reached your family.

Theodore:

- Thank you, Pierre. Yes, my family loved your gifts.

Pierre:

- Glad to hear that. I am happy to keep providing for your family if you can help me spread public health awareness. I have come up with a great breakthrough.

Theodore:

- Promoting public health is the basis for my entire organisation. Please share your findings with me, Pierre.

Pierre:

- Estimates based on serological testing infer that billions of people are infected by dormant Hei Bai Virus.

Theodore:

- Yes, I saw those studies. The same study also showed that one has to eat a lot of selenium to activate the virus. That's never going to happen unless there is a new bioweapon attack.

Pierre:

- But what if I showed you, that dormant Hei Bai virus can break out without an excessive selenium intake?

Theodore:

- It can't. We haven't had any cases where a high selenium intake wasn't involved.

Pierre:

- Correct. But what if I pay some scientists to publish a fake study claiming that? Meanwhile, I'll fill all media with terrifying imagery from the New York and Xuwan outbreaks.

- Furthermore, I want you and the GHA to release terrifying statements about the new findings.

Theodore:

- Why would you benefit from this?

Pierre:

- Because I have released a new drug to cure the Hei Bai virus. A proprietary molecule of Ammonium molybdate tetrahydrate. The drug will contain the equivalent of 1mg of Molybdenum.

Having said this, Pierre handed Theodore a document. Theodore read the document for a while and replied:

- That's five times the upper limit for daily molybdenum intake. Such high levels could cause liver damage and infertility.

Pierre:

- But it does cure the Hei Bai Virus.

Theodore:

- Yes. But considering how easy it is to not trigger a dormant Hei Bai virus infection, this cure is a lot worse than the disease.

Pierre:

- Exactly and that's the purpose of any drug.

- If a drug has dangerous side effects, which another drug can reduce, one has created an endless spiral of drug use. That's great for business!

Theodore:

- That's very cynical.

Pierre:

- Funny that the man who covered up the first case of Hei Bai virus, is criticising morals. I know what you did, Theodore.

Theodore:

- There is a nice mansion in your neighbourhood that is up for sale...

Pierre:

- I can organise that.

- But you must be starving. Let's head to a nice restaurant and celebrate Global Health efforts!

Having said this, Pierre led Theodore out of his office. Pierre felt excited about the new evil plan that would make him even wealthier and his malicious grin couldn't leave his ugly face!

Chapter 37: Epilogue.

Pierre and Theodore carried out their plan and they promoted Pierre's dangerous drug. The drug did cure the dormant Hei Bai virus but it also caused half a million people to die worldwide from liver damages, and it caused another 50 million people to become infertile. Due to Pierre's and Theodore's grip of the world's governments, the information about the side effects never became public knowledge.

For the next two decades, Pierre kept coming up with evil schemes in his endless desire to increase his wealth. Justice reached Pierre in 2040 as Sabina Hines killed him when he was plotting to start a civil war in Mexico.

Likewise, Vladimir Kravchenko and James Winter fell victims to Sabina Hines' quest to stop the Monocle Conspiracy in 2040.

Biyu Sang emigrated to Switzerland and spent her life working a high-paying position with the World Bank. The bullet that went through her shoulder during the escape from China made her unable to use that arm. However, all in all, she led a happy life and raised a happy family.

Eileen Lu was very vengeful against her former enemies in the Columnist Party. During the trials for the Xuwan outbreak, she decided to execute every member of the previous national parliament. The trial led to the execution of over 2000 Columnist Party leaders, many of them innocent to Jing Xi's genocidal plans. The execution of the 2000 most prominent Chinese leaders crashed the Chinese economy. This was because many of them had a large amount of money hidden in overseas accounts. Eileen and the Chinese government could never find and access these monies.

Since Eileen's actions caused an economic collapse in China, her popularity crashed and a peaceful protest ousted her a few years later. Eileen went into exile overseas, and she married a Chinese businessman who died when she was 50.

A few years later, she rekindled her flame with Jared and they stayed together until the end.

Jared Pond separated from Eileen Lu in 2022 as he realised that power had gone to her head and she had become the very evil that she had set out to stop. After leaving Eileen, Jared hunted down Greg Steel and brought him to justice for his involvement with Jing Xi. After bringing Greg to justice, Jared spent many years philandering, gambling and drinking. Finally, at the age of 60, Jared reconnected with Eileen who had been ousted from power, many years earlier. Once Eileen was not in a position of power, she turned into the same woman that Jared fell in love with. They stayed together until death did them apart, 20 years later.

The End

Please check out **The Fall of Martin Orchard** and **Sabina Saves the Future** that involves several of the characters from this book.

Don't miss out!

Visit the website below and you can sign up to receive emails whenever Martin Lundqvist publishes a new book. There's no charge and no obligation.

https://books2read.com/r/B-A-QIOG-MNTFB

BOOKS2READ

Connecting independent readers to independent writers.

Also by Martin Lundqvist

Divine Space Gods
Divine Space Gods: Abraham's Follies
Divine Space Gods II: Revolution for Dummies
Divine Space Gods III: Rangda's Shenanigans

Sabina Saves the Future
Sabina's Pursuit of The Holy Grail
Sabina's Quest to Open the Portal in the Sun Pyramid
Sabina's Expedition to Stop the Apocalypse

The Divine Zetan Trilogy
The Divine Dissimulation
The Divine Sedition
The Divine Finalisation

Standalone
Matt's Amazing Week
James Locker The Duality of Fate
The Portal in the Pyramid
Money Laundering in the Laundromat
Pyramidportalen

Matts Fantastiska Vecka
Divine Space Gods Trilogy
Sabina Saves the Future: Complete Trilogy
Diez Historias Aleatorias y Muy Cortas
Ten Random and Very Short Stories
Dieci Storie Casuali e Molto Brevi
Dix Histoires Aléatoires et Très Courtes
Zehn Zufällige und Sehr Kurze Geschichten
Cinco Historias Aleatorias y Muy Cortas
Five Random and Very Short Stories
The Fall of Martin Orchard
Masa Depan Putri Sabina
La Caída de Martin Orchard
The Banker and The Dragon

Watch for more at martinlundqvist.com.